I0744962

Ere's Secret
&
223 Bonny Street
by
FIRI KAMSON

Ere's Secret

First Published in Great Britain in 2019 by
LOVE AFRICA PRESS
103 Reaver House, 12 East Street, Epsom KT17
1HX
www.loveafricapress.com

LOVE AFRICA
PRESS
African Love Stories

Text copyright © Firi Kamson, 2015

ISBN 978-1-9164755-8-8
Also available as ebook

DEDICATION

Growing up, writing has always been a part of me. This is, if you count the numerous dairies I had over the years. I never really thought I would transition into writing books, but here I am with two short stories. It's scary and crazy that this is going to be published and people all over the world would be able to have access to this book. I hope you all like it as I have loved writing it. I am sure I would go ahead and write numerous stories and novels and romantic nonsense, but Ere's Secret and 223, Bonny Street would forever be dear to my heart.

I'll like to dedicate this book to my very dear friend who is my sister from another mother, Titilopemi Adanne Owoyemi. Getting to know you in Brunei was just the best thing I could have hoped for, because before I got there, I wouldn't have guessed that far away from home, a sister would be found. Thank you for pushing me to write all the time and taking the time to read and read my writings.

I cannot publish this book without speaking about my grandfather, Titus Tamunomoni Green, the actually owner of 223, Bonny Street. He was the best grandfather one could ever ask for and a fantastic priest. He also showed me what it really was to love a woman and be in love with her 'til death do you part.

I'll like to thank Kiru Taye for thinking of me. It's amazing what she is doing with Love Africa Press. Make sure you all follow her handle on Instagram and Facebook.

Thank you, Zee, for your patience and just being there, making sure this author gets it right.

Lastly, Temi, thank you for truly loving me and staying true to your promise.

Ere's Secret
by
FIRI KAMSON

BLURB

I have a secret. In three days, I'll be turning forty, and I'm in love for the first time. Decades ago, I sacrificed my life for the good of my family. But tragedy struck too close to home, reminding me of the brevity of life. Now, I have a choice to make: continue living in the shadows, or allow my true self to emerge.

22ⁿᵈ December, 2014.
Rainy Season. Three days to go.
Dear Diary,

My name is Erewarifagha Green, but everyone calls me Ere. I am from a small village called Green's Iwoama, in the heart of Grand Bonny Kingdom, which is an island partly famous for being a great gateway for foreign trade centuries ago. With its rich cultural heritage and dynamic culture, it is a place I will always hold dear to my heart.

Nonetheless, in three days, I will be turning forty, and I am in love. So, I am going to have a small birthday celebration and will reveal to all my friends and family my little secret. I know what they will likely say, as I have tried to tell them a few details—just as an old African man will behave when he gives his grown children advice hidden in the heart of parables. You know what I mean, right?

I have tried to make them understand discreetly, just as you enclose your child's poop carefully within the soiled diaper, so it doesn't spill and make a mess.

Yes! I carefully wrapped the words, hoping they would understand what I was saying and get to know me as a person a bit more, not just as the mother of Inye or the wife of Opuada. But they didn't get it. All they understood was only what their narrow minds allowed them to.

It's a bit scary, and sometimes, I just want to back off and crawl into my shell again, which is ordinarily what I would have done. But then, I think of my mother, and I am sure she will swear on her late father's grave that me, her daughter, Ere, will never be involved in anything like this.

Well, after all I have done for her and my siblings, I am hoping she will overlook this and just try to understand where I stand. I have been the breadwinner of my family, way before Opuada and even after Opuada. My brothers were sponsored to the university, with the hopes that when they graduate, they would in turn make sure all their other siblings, me included, will be well taken care of.

But where are they now? My first brother, Boma, my mother's first fruit, ended up being a school drop-out. I can't begin to start telling you his story, so let's just leave it at that.

I have told my mother he is a lost cause, but she won't listen. She keeps running from one pastor to the other, for prayers that the demon responsible for her son's irresponsibility will be cast out pronto and leave her son in peace. Needless to say, no luck there yet.

My second brother, Tonye, went to school, graduated, started practicing medicine, and is now quite wealthy, but has run off to the United States of America, married a White American woman so that he can get an American passport, and has forgotten his family in Nigeria. A family who sold almost everything they had so that he could attend medical school.

Like I said, I am hoping that my mother will remember all the good I have done for her. Right from the surgery of his enlarged prostate that my father had to undergo at the Port Harcourt Teaching hospital that was all hush hush, because it's kind of like a cultural taboo for a man to let on that he has a problem with his manhood, so he is not classified as a woman or half-man amongst his circle of friends. To when my mother had to have an emergency hysterectomy, because the pressure of having too many kids had almost killed her—the doctor said the only solution was to remove her ovaries and uterus.

I was there by her side, paying the bills and housing all my siblings for months 'til she recovered. I also footed their own bills and endured their self-indulgent demands on end. I hope she remembers all this, even though I know in my heart of hearts, this may be just false hope on my part. But still, I hope.

My dear, I can see Musa, the gateman, from my bedroom window. I can see him coming out of his cubicle, and he is probably getting ready for his prayers. I can also see Peace just coming into the house. Oh, yes, I sent her to get me Sister Clara's *piom piom* as this may be the last time I taste it for a very long time.

Ahhh, Sister Clara's *piom pioms* are the best. I always salivate any time I see the dish. In a small calabash, you behold the black, rough backs of little pieces of something that looks like bugs in the eyes of a stranger. 'Til you pick it up with your fingers and suck on it, *oh la la la,* the juicy periwinkle comes tumbling into your mouth. Rolling it on your tongue, you chew it, taking in the hot spice mixed with stir-fried palm oil sauce. Yes, today may be the last time I taste this *piom piom* for a long time. You still do not understand, my dear, do you?

I know, my friend, you feel I am out of my mind. I feel the same, as well; that I may be out of my mind, but I know I am doing the right thing. For the first time in my life, I am doing something for myself, not something to please anyone else but myself. I know I am in a hurry to pour it all out there because I want it all to be revealed, but the truth is, I really do not know how to begin.

Hold on, I can hear a knock at the door. It must be Peace with my *piom piom*. Let me go off now. I will chat with you later after I have devoured it.

22nd December, 2014.

8 p.m.

Dear Diary,

My dear, I am back again. I am so sorry—I got caught up in a lot of activities. I know I promised to come back immediately after I finished my *piom piom,* but I had a visitor. Sister Ibelema came to see me, and as usual, she wanted something from me. This lady has always wanted something from me right from the time I got married to her brother 'til today.

Now, let's get back to the basics a bit. You know ten years ago, I became a widow. Yes, it has been ten years. I mourned my husband like a dutiful wife, like a woman in love, but you know, you wouldn't blame me; I didn't know any better.

At that time, I had convinced myself that I was in love with my husband, and it was my duty to mourn him. Instead of wearing the traditional white for one year, I insisted on wearing it for two years, to the delight of my in-laws, and they loved it. I never understood why they derived joy in seeing me sad. They kept on telling me to keep their brother's image alive in my heart and in the hearts of my children. I did all that.

Don't get me wrong—I will never deprive my kids of having a good memory of their father, even though I know they know that he wasn't the saint his sisters painted him to be.

But what was I to do?

That was all I knew at the time. Whenever I tried to complain, I was shut up. After all, everybody said it was in his house I became who I am today. This is not true. Yes, I married very early, which is my past, and I cannot change it. I had just finished Finima Girls, the secondary school I attended on Bonny Island, by the age of fifteen, which was very young as most of my classmates were aged about twenty at their graduation. But I was lucky to begin school early because my father was the principal of the school at the time.

I loved school, and I had thought that maybe I would become a doctor, or nurse. I knew it was going to be a big toll on my father as I had nine siblings: six sisters and three brothers.

My two older brothers had left the house. Like I said, the first one, Boma, was a lost cause, as he spent his time chasing everything in skirts, joining the local masquerade group, performing with them all the time, and always looking for his next fix while my other brother, Tonye, was in the U.S., and even though I felt there wasn't any redemption for my brother Boma, I still loved him a lot. He always had wonderful stories to tell when sober and whenever he came back from his trips, as he sometimes worked as a deck-hand.

I loved him dearly, but I knew that he was a heartbreaker; the icing on the cake was that he was one of the most handsome men I have ever laid my eyes on, and so I do not blame the women who swooned around him, or the two women who gave birth to my nephews a week apart.

Being the next in line as the third born and the first daughter, I was bestowed with the noble task of being the upright child and daughter. My father, God rest his soul, would spend his weekends fishing, all in a bid to boost his miserly salary.

On good days, he would come back with a canoe full of fish, and my mother and I would hurriedly take them to the market hoping that it would be a good sale for us. I always believed I had the Midas touch, as whenever we were at the market, customers would gravitate towards our table and buy up everything.

This is what we used to run our large family, as my mother didn't know what family planning was. She always said that she was going to give birth to all the babies in her womb as the Good Lord will permit her, so she was literarily giving birth every other year. In addition to my nine siblings, my mother had lost two children at birth.

I really wished she would stop turning our house into a breeding ground, but I couldn't voice that opinion out because, according to her, it was a woman's lot to have as many children as she could, especially sons, because male children were a woman's security in her husband's house. So when my mother wasn't busy giving birth to children or taking care of the little ones, she was in the market trying to sell off the fish my father brought home during the weekends.

My dear friend, with all this responsibility, I decided, or rather, my family decided, that I was to go to Port Harcourt, to stay with my father's first cousin who was married to a very wealthy politician, as she had promised my father she would take care of my tuition.

So, although I was scared about leaving Bonny for the first time—after all, that was all I knew—I realized that if I wanted more in life, I had to travel away from home, even if it was to the next village. Finally, the time came when I bid my parents farewell, and with my new cloth bag, given to me by Sofiri, my best friend's mother, I was on the early morning local speed boat to Port Harcourt.

Goodness, it is now about midnight. We shall continue tomorrow. Good night.

23ʳᵈ December, 2014.
In the bedroom. 6 a.m.
Dear Diary,

I am lying on my back now, staring at this ceiling, I cannot believe that my birthday is in two days. I love my birthday, 25ᵗʰ December. The 25ᵗʰ of December was the only day my auntie, Auntie Mina, the one married to the rich politician, remembered to give me a proper meal. Or so I like to think, but I think she actually gave me a proper meal because it was also Christmas Day and she always had a lot of guests come over.

Thinking back, my trip to Port Harcourt happened in a daze. Even though it was such a long time ago, I remember it like it was yesterday. I can still smell the salt water sea, and I remember when the boat started, and as it sped off, I kept looking back at my mother and all my siblings who had walked with me to the waterside to bid me farewell.

I kept remembering all the advice she gave me and all her prayers. She told me everything a good girl should do and prayed that I would, like my auntie, marry a rich man who would help rescue my family from poverty.

I kept on looking back until all I could see were the large expanse of the sea and the mangrove trees with their branches almost falling into the water and the occasional monkeys that jumped up and down as they tried to hide from humans.

The lady who was given the task of taking me to my Auntie Mina's house noticed I was a bit apprehensive. For the purpose of this story, I will call her Patience, because in all honesty, I never knew her name. Tapping me on the back, she tried in her own way to tell me to relax, saying that I was very lucky, as life had just dealt me the greatest favour ever: a wealthy auntie to become my benefactor.

No more worries in life.

And I believed it all.

I was ready to do anything to please this auntie. From the stories I heard, my father's cousin's life had changed the moment she'd met her husband. She had even built a storeyed building in the village and in Bonny main town for her father. Her father frequently boasted of his son in-law's generosity.

I had been told by my father that Auntie Mina used to come to Bonny frequently when I was younger, but I must admit, my father said she looked exactly like him, and that the resemblance was very striking. I didn't believe him, though, because he was the only odd-looking member of his family. I was yet to see anybody who looked anything like him, apart from his children.

When I got to the Bonny waterside in Port Harcourt, I was stuck by the filth. I couldn't imagine that one end of the waterside could be dirty and the other end which was the Bonny angle could be clean. The amount of people I saw terrified me, as well. There were all sorts of *agberos*, local touts hanging around, struggling to grab any unfortunate passenger's bag and automatically charge them for their services.

Since I didn't have much, I wasn't considered a meal ticket and was left alone, and I had kept my bag on my thighs all through the journey. Following as quickly as I could, I walked briskly behind Patience, my surrogate guardian at that moment. I joined her as we hailed a taxi and got inside. She kept on looking at me like she had just struck gold, and she kept emphasizing my good fortune, warning me not to waste the opportunity, as my auntie was helping me not become like most of the girls in the village, who just sat at home and had children for useless men.

I was still afraid and scared of what the future held, but I kept my mouth shut and didn't say a word. I just looked around as I saw different houses, a lot of them unlike what I was familiar with.

Port Harcourt in my view wasn't like Bonny. It was bigger, dirtier, noisier, with wider roads, buildings everywhere, and numerous cars of different models. In Bonny, one could count the cars, as we had just one major, tarred road. In fact, it was only very few people who had cars, mostly people who worked with the international companies, and there were very few of them who competed with the motorcyclists on the road.

I listened to the taxi driver as he bemoaned the influx of motor bikes or *Okada*, as they were commonly called in the town, which were used as a form of transportation. I found it odd that the taxi driver, who was a Yoruba man—clearly not an indigene of the state, as his colleagues called him Papa Seun, with all his facial tribal marks—would come to a state that wasn't his and complain about other outsiders coming into the area to destroy it with their unruly driving. But like I said, I kept my mouth shut as a mouse and watched.

I could see houses of all kinds, big and small. People jostling for transportation while others walked leisurely like they didn't have any care in the world. The highway, which the driver called Aba Express Road, was very wide; it was a three-lane road.

In retrospect, though, it wasn't as wide as I had thought it was at that time. Imagine me seeing only a one-lane road all my life, and all of a sudden, I was thrown into a city that had a three-lane highway, like a new-born baby emerging into the world. Do you blame a small, village girl like me for my grand imaginings?

After what seemed like a very long drive, we turned into a residential area which looked extremely quiet with big houses, lovely greenery, and huge fences which obscured the beauty of most of the houses. The driver again explained to us that this was the exclusive abode of the wealthy. He proceeded to state that if anyone wanted to pay a visit to any of the residents, they would be delayed by the security guards for hours on end, before they could see the *Oga* or Madam of the house.

I hoped this wasn't going to be our own dilemma, as the sky was already showing signs of rain. I knew it wasn't going to look good meeting my auntie for the first time resembling a frightened, wet little mouse.

Papa Seun isn't someone you forget in a hurry because from the beginning of the journey 'til the time we got to our destination, he didn't stop talking. He even hiked up the cab fare the moment he saw the address.

This didn't ruffle Patience as she confidently told him that the madam of the house was going to pay. Contrary to what Papa Seun said, we didn't wait outside the gate for hours, but were ushered in immediately, shocking Papa Seun, who had asked the gateman twice if it was okay to come in as he was directed to the parking area.

Oh, wow, I have already spent an hour with you. I have to leave now. Later.

23rd December, 2014.
9 p.m.
Dear Diary,

I am back, oh. You know, I also have to attend to personal needs. So where did I stop? Okay, when we got to my Auntie's house.

My dear, the house was the finest thing I had ever seen. It was really huge. I began to wonder how someone could live in a house so big with just one child. Where we lived in Bonny, my parents and ten children, was a match box compared to this house.

The driveway seemed as long as an endless maze. It curved into a large garage with different models of cars. Cars I had never seen before in my life, from small ones to huge, gigantic vehicles, and so, as though Papa Seun was scared of having an accident, he parked his beat-up cab far away from the cars, not wanting to be responsible for anything untoward happening. For the first time since the journey began, he was short of words.

Left and right, there were different trees, with the only ones I could identify being the palm trees. By the side of the house, I saw flowers, roses of different colours; at least, I could identify a rose. I had seen it countless times in one of the textbooks Mr. Smart, one of my secondary school teachers, forced us to read before we took any national exams, even though it never helped in solving the tough exam questions, as the books and the questions were usually worlds apart in content.

Quietly, we came out of the car, and I followed Patience, like a sheep following its shepherd. I waited as she rang the bell while I tried not to look around so much, even though from her reaction, I could tell that this probably was the first time she was coming to a house like this.

Within seconds, the door was opened by someone who was dressed in a checked blue and white A-line dress, which looked like a uniform, and a matching head scarf. Saying good afternoon, she opened the door even wider and ushered us into what seemed like a waiting room, with instructions to wait there as her madam was going to be with us shortly. Even though the sofas were a dark shade of blue, we, Patience and I, both refrained from sitting down on it, as we didn't want to stain the sofas with our dirty clothes. Opposite the love seat, there was a wooden shelf, made out of beautiful, dark wood.

I never knew what kind of wood that was. The only wood I was familiar with was wood gotten from the oak tree, and so, I assumed the shelf was made out of oak. The shelf had drawers, and on top of it were lit huge candles, which I later learnt were called scented candles, which made the house smell very nice. There were three fantastic figurines, also on top of the shelf.

One that caught my eye was the figurine of a sea horse. I knew it was a sea horse, as during one of my father's numerous fishing trips, he'd accidentally caught a sea horse. My dad had thrown it away, as he said it wasn't eaten by Bonny people. I'd taken it out from the bin, dried it a bit under the fire, and kept it. I loved the little creature. It was my very own little pet even though it was dead, and the day I eventually lost it, I cried as I felt like I had lost a dear friend.

The most striking thing in the room was the huge, golden-framed family portrait of my auntie, her husband, and their son. What struck me was that her husband was one of the ugliest men I had ever seen, and I wondered how she could have married him, but seeing this house, I didn't have to worry my head too much.

My first meeting with my auntie was very *comme si, comme ça*. I tried to decipher her character, but she was a very hard person to read. She was all so chatty and happy to see me, hugged me and gave me a kiss, saying all the time that she was happy to see me and had been waiting for me for a long time. She asked my guide, Patience, how the journey was, and then as though on cue, brought out a brown envelope and gave her.

From the huge smile on Patience's face, I could tell that it was more than enough for the taxi fare. Then turning towards me, Patience smilingly pinched her ears in emphasis, as she told me to make sure I was very good to my auntie and remained an obedient girl as this was an opportunity given to me on a platter of gold.

I thanked her and watched her go. A part of me wanted to run after her and beg her not to leave me in this strange big house, as she was the only familiar face I knew, but I just stared after her 'til she had left, dazed.

My auntie, Auntie Mina, called out a name I was familiar with, Imabong. One of my childhood friends was also called Imabong, and the uniformed lady who'd opened the door for us quickly came in and listened to my auntie instruct her to take me to my room and give me something to eat.

A statement she made that I will never forget was that I was to sleep in one of the rooms downstairs, as I was family.

I followed her through a wide corridor, looking left and right, making a conscious point of not touching the walls, as I didn't want to stain the shiny white surfaces.

Walking with my bare feet, it dawned on me that this house was very clean. I couldn't feel any grain of sand under my feet, and upon stepping into my allocated room, I almost passed out. This room was bigger than the two-bedroom zinc house my parents and siblings lived in, in Bonny. The bed was so huge, and listening to the uniformed lady telling me that my toilet and bathroom was behind a closed door, I laughed to myself. I was going to have my own room, my own toilet and bathroom. This was luxury.

Up until this time, I had never thought that there were people in this same country, Nigeria, who lived this way.

Putting my things down on the floor beside the bed, I quickly followed the uniformed lady into the kitchen and silently ate the boiled yam and egg stew that she served me on a glass plate. That day, I made a new friend, a friend also named Imabong.

24th December, 2014.
Dry Season. 11 a.m.
Dear Diary,
My friendship with Imabong, the uniformed maid, was bittersweet as she often told me things I didn't want to hear.

In a matter of days, I realized that my Auntie Mina wasn't a likable person. All the welcome hugging and smiling had been just a façade. Yes, I was family, but I was treated like trash, which I didn't mind, as to me, this was still the best opportunity ever.

I was told that I was going to be sent to the university if I was a hardworking student, but all that didn't happen. Instead, I was sent to learn how to sew, which I detested with a passion. Since Imabong and the cook, Charles, were in charge of feeding, from grocery shopping to the preparation of the meals, I was never hungry, but my auntie was the meanest woman ever. She had frequent mood swings, and whenever she had a quarrel with her husband, she poured out her frustration on me. And it was a constant in the house, because whenever the boss was around, they were always arguing. The only person I felt sorry for was their son.

At the time I came to stay with my auntie, he was four years old, and by the time I left her house, he was six and half. He cried when I left, because I had become his surrogate mother. I did everything for him which his mother never had the time to do.

She said she was always busy, but busy doing what? I can't say. All I can say is that she was the wife of a rich politician. 'Til today, I often wonder what his life turned out to be, because he was a child thirsty for parental attention and affection. His father just saw him as his child, a male to keep the family name going, and my auntie saw him as a nuisance.

Often times when she was probably drunk, she would say things like she knows that if she hadn't had a male child, she would have been thrown away from her husband's house a long time ago. And yes, remember that my Auntie's husband was the ugliest man ever, and very proud. He was uglier in person than in the framed picture, and he was also very short. He was a lecherous, philandering man, so I made sure I kept my room door locked at all times.

Truthfully, living in my Auntie's house was a nightmare, and I had to find an escape route. This led to my impromptu marriage to Opuada. Auntie Mina was very angry with me because Opuada was her younger brother's friend. She called me a gold digger, saying that it had been my design all along to snag myself a rich, unsuspecting old man, thanking her stars that her husband, being a saint, hadn't fallen prey to my Jezebellian allure.

I laughed. My auntie was either clueless or living in denial. Why did she think I always had my room door locked?

Well, I didn't set out to marry a rich old man; it just happened. Opuada said all the sweet things I wanted to hear, and I fancied myself in love with him. With the pressure from my parents to send them money, I conditioned my mind to believe that I had found my true love, and so, I married Opuada.

Did I have everything I wanted? Yes, I did.

My dear, at the time I married Opuada, I was eighteen years old. In fact, I conceived my first son the first day we made love. Don't ask me about the experience as it was horrible; that was my first time.

He kept on telling me not to worry and that it will get better, but it never did.

My wedding celebration was a very elaborate one, which was celebrated in my hometown, Bonny. Because my father wanted to show off to his friends that his daughter was getting married to a wealthy man, he insisted I was to do my *Ira Bibite*.

I loved the *Ira Bibite* festival, a very colourful, interesting coming into womanhood festival in the Bonny kingdom, which can be very expensive, and I didn't want all that burden on Opuada. But like my father, he, too, didn't mind showing off, and so, we went ahead with the *Ira Bibite* ceremony. I was dressed up in different arrays of wrappers, blouses, and jewellery, and was told not to speak the whole day. Whenever I was outside dancing to the beat of the drums played by the skilful drummers, I remained mute, only smiling as I danced.

Dancing was something I knew how to do, and the more I danced gracefully like a queen, the more Opuada and his friends sprayed me with different currencies from Naira to Dollars, and the more my sisters who were assigned the task of picking up the money scrambled on the floor, under the watchful eyes of my mother.

After my *Ira Bibite* came the traditional marriage. I was first bathed in something called *Uri,* which is a reddish substance usually mixed with palm oil, to remove all dead skin and make my body glow, my ebony complexion shining as bright as the stars. Then, they used *Uhie,* which was used to make designs on my body. When my mother insisted that the designs must last a long time on my body, the women used *Edeala,* which was semi-permanent. This stayed on my skin months after the wedding, but I didn't mind, as I loved it.

Oh, yes, I was forced to eat a heavy breakfast of boiled yam and spicy dried fish pepper soup, which almost took me straight to bed, but I couldn't as I had to be awake while the women worked judiciously.

I loved the ceremony, everything about it, even though I was clad in heavy wrappers to add bulk to my frame because I was deemed skinny with no buttocks and no hips; very unlike the typical Bonny woman. Because of this, I had five wrappers underneath the outer wrapper, thereafter creating an effect, like magic, of a woman with the desired curves. I had dancers whom I followed and danced gracefully. I looked like a queen who had everything taken care of and was spoilt rotten by her subjects.

But deep down, I was afraid of this new road.

Everyone told me how lucky I was.

Everyone blessed me and prayed for me.

My aunties prayed that their daughters would be just like me when they grew up. My husband-to-be, Opuada, was my family's saviour, and therefore, he was treated like a king. Like a man who could do no wrong.

I could see him smiling proudly to his friends when I came out clad in the outfits he had bought for me. I could see my mother beaming with joy and making sure everybody knew that the wrapper, blouse, gold jewellery, and corals she was wearing were gifts from her new son-in-law. Oh, my father, clad in his *etibo* and wrapper, boasted to his friends that since his son-in-law came into his life, he had ceased wasting his time fishing.

Why are you giggling? Because I said wrapper? Yes, Bonny men tie wrappers, which are called *George*.

When I asked my mother why they tied wrappers instead of wearing trousers, she told me that long ago during her forefathers' times when we didn't have jetties built, we relied solely on the tides.

So, when the tides came in, we quickly ran into our canoes and paddled away. And when the tides ebbed, we raised our wrappers and walked slowly through the *atuma*, black muddy quicksand, to get into the waiting canoes so as not to allow oneself be swallowed by it. With trousers, this would have almost been an impossible task.

I wished my father would not stop fishing. I wished my mother would stop talking about the saviour she saw in my soon-to-be husband. I wished they didn't put all their trust in him, but then, there was nothing I could do.

So, I watched Opuada beam with pride seeing me, his bride, and I smiled, knowing that my destiny was irrevocably tied to him.

24th December, 2014.
12.30 p.m.
Dear Diary,

My dear friend, like I said earlier, after all my ordeals with my auntie and her husband, I got married to Opuada when I was eighteen years old. At the time we got married, he was already thirty-five years old. Yes, the age gap between us was seventeen years.

At first, I didn't mind, because I could understand his plight. He, too, was the oldest in his family, and he had had to struggle all his life to become someone and had been given the task of taking care of his other siblings.

Fortunately, his mum didn't have a whole village of children like my mum did; he only had three sisters. The downside of it was that his mum raised him with the mentality that he was God's gift to the world. He was king in his house, and whatever he said was considered gold.

So like I said earlier, at first when we got married, I didn't mind the age difference, but along the line, I began to see that we were worlds apart in thinking and reasoning. In fact, we were generations apart.

You know when technology just started seeping into the country little by little, he resisted the change. He felt that the *Oyibo* had come with their witchcraft to deceive us again, as they had during the colonial era.

I couldn't believe that a man who had become rich through sheer hard work refused to embrace the change. He was a very good business man, as he was one of the only few who controlled most of the private speed boats at the jetty that plied the Bonny-Port Harcourt route.

His business increased further with the influx of the establishment of international companies on Bonny Island, since he was one of the few who introduced the speed boats, which reduced the journey time from many hours to just about an hour. This was a blessing, as people could go in and out of Bonny any time, meaning that he was gone most weekends, and on weekdays, he was at the office all the time.

Did I have a husband? Yes, I did.

Did I have a personal relationship with my husband?

I will say for the average Nigerian woman, yes, I did. From my mother's testimony, I did have a fantastic husband because any time she came to Port Harcourt, she always rained praises on him. She loved the house. She would always scold my younger siblings not to sit on the white sofas so as not to dirty them, and even when I insisted that it wasn't an issue, when I gave them the three rooms downstairs, she insisted that they only use one room.

Yes, looking at my life, I had everything.

Because I had married Opuada, my siblings all got the opportunity to complete their education.

Because of Opuada, my parents got a stipend every month.

Because of Opuada, my family moved from a two-bedroom match box house made of zinc to a modern, five-bedroom bungalow.

My parents and siblings actually had proper beds to sleep on, and thank God because of the last complication my mother had when she was having her eighth child or was it her ninth—I can't remember any more—she was strongly advised not to have any more children.

So yes, I should be thankful that Opuada had brought light into my family.

But what about me?

I was everything a wife could be.

He always had freshly made soup and *Garri* waiting for him whenever he came back from work. Opuada was the kind of man who wanted everything freshly made by his wife, so even though I wasn't a farmer, I had to learn to make *Garri* from scratch, from getting the cassava, to frying the *garri*—I learnt the whole process, because he was a man who loved his swallows.

His house was very clean and always smelt nice. I never wasted his money and always kept the receipts of whatever I purchased. I was the perfect wife, and yes, I took all the crap his sisters dished out because I think that deep down, they were jealous of me.

They always made remarks like I spent all their brother's money and never left anything for them, which was a lie. Since I had always been used to pinching pennies, I was very good with savings. Thankfully, Opuada wasn't that controlling, so I had my own bank account where I saved every month, no matter how little.

I couldn't complain, but then, I did. At this point, I had been married for seven years; I was twenty-five years old, and I had three boys aged six, five, and four. Yes, I had them one after the other, which may not have been the wisest decision, but then, everyone said I was a strong woman and that was my lot in life.

Secretly, though, after my third son, I went on the pill. I had vowed early in life never to be like my mother, because in my opinion, three children were enough for one woman, and since Opuada and I had separate rooms and separate bathrooms, it was easy for me to keep my pills safely hidden, away from his prying eyes.

Yes, I was twenty-five years old, and I wanted more.

I wanted to be more than a mother and a wife.

I wanted to do something more for myself.

I think I had gotten to this point where I was tired of depending on a man.

In the beginning, this was the only way I knew, but time had shown me it wasn't the only way. I saw women everywhere all looking classy, confident, determined, and with a purpose as they worked. They earned a living. They had children, and yes, some of them were married, too. Whenever I went to the village, I would see my friends who always begged me to help them find a husband like Opuada so they, too, could have all the good things of life that I was enjoying. I wanted to tell them that marriage should not be the ultimate goal of a woman. That, at least, they should spend their single years discovering their inner selves.

But I couldn't.

Telling them that would have meant betraying my wedding vows, or the institution of marriage as we knew it. It would have portrayed me as a very selfish, ungrateful woman after all I had received from my husband.

When I finally summoned the courage to tell Opuada that I wanted to go to the university, he laughed, jokingly telling me that I was going to waste his money like his sisters who were blockheads. I told him that I wasn't a blockhead and that in Bonny, I had always been the best in my class, but he refused.

He asked what course I wanted to study. I said Theatre Arts. This brought a good laugh and some insults. He said that I wanted to go and follow men, or better still, become a prostitute like all my village friends who were dating one foreigner or the other, simply for material gains. When I asked what studying Theatre Arts had to do with prostituting, he quickly shouted that I should never question his authority again, and so, the matter was buried under the carpet.

Note that Opuada was a very responsible husband, but he was of the opinion that a wife stayed submissive at all cost, and all desires she emitted were to please her husband and no one else. It was later I discovered why Opuada didn't want me to go to school; it was because he was a university dropout. My getting a degree was only going to magnify his insecurities, and so I stayed at home, year in, year out, playing the role of big madam while I died within.

Do I sense you wonder about my boys? Yes, I loved them; I still love them, very much, too. I look at them today, and I know that they are different. My first son, Inye, is like his father. He thinks the world revolves around him and he is God's gift to women. I love him still. I tried not to instil this kind of mentality in him, but his father would not hear of it. Whenever as a little boy he cried, his father would beat him black and blue for crying, telling him that men do not cry for any reason, ending up calling him a woman wrapper.

I watched Inye mature into a hard man with little feelings as young as eight years old. I cried all the time when I saw him this way, but I love him. He is twenty-two years old now, through with school and recently returned from America, in time for me to reveal my big secret. I know if there is any one of my boys who will not forgive me, it will be him.

My second and third sons, Abel and Adonye, will probably try to act all angry like their older brother, but they will come around in time, because they always want to see me happy. I will have to explain to them why I have chosen this path, even though I feel they understand a little bit of why I am doing this.

They have very soft hearts, especially Adonye, who is Mummy's little helper. Growing up, he loved to be in the kitchen with me. Helping me cook, bake, everything he wanted to learn. He always told me that he wanted to be a chef, but his father squashed that idea, as in his books, kitchens were meant for women only.

My dear friend, I know you want to know what my secret is, but I will have to start from where it all began. Oh, yes, it's coming. Unfortunately or fortunately, any way you want to look at it, Opuada died after eleven years of our marriage, and I was twenty-nine years old then. It was surprising and surreal. He left for Bonny on Friday morning, which was his weekly routine, to be back on Sunday. And this particular Sunday evening at about the same time Opuada usually came into the house, the doorbell rang.

Mary, my maid at that time, came in to tell me that some visitors had come to see me, and it was very urgent. When I got into the parlour, I remember thinking to myself that the room with its white furnishings had never looked as cold as it looked that day, making a note to convince Opuada that we had to change the chairs as I was tired of scrubbing them white. Then, I saw the look on *Warisenibo* Jumbo's face, and it was at that moment that I realized that for a leader in the Jumbo House of Grand Bonny to be in my house, something drastic had happened.

Something indeed had. My husband Opuada had drowned in a boat accident. Sadly and ironically, in all the years of running a boat business, Opuada had never learnt how to swim or insist that his passengers use life jackets whenever they were on the sea, as safety wasn't his strong concern; he had a God complex, and this led to his untimely death.

I cried as the dutiful wife, for yes, I knew I was going to miss him. He was all I knew. I hadn't even taken in the sad news properly when I heard the footsteps of my in-laws. They had come to claim everything their brother had in the guise of mourning.

Well, thankfully, their brother had been sharper than they thought and had made arrangements for his belongings to be equitably distributed. Burial arrangements were made, and like in the movies, Opuada was given a proper Christian burial even though the last time he set foot in a church was during Inye's christening.

When his body was lowered to the ground, I cuddled my boys. Inye, the oldest, refused to be wrapped around my hands as he wanted to show the men that he was a man, but my other boys, Abel and Adonye, sat down beside me and cried. I wailed, not because I had been head over heels in love with him, but because I just couldn't imagine life without him.

What was I to do?

All I knew in life was being a mother and taking instructions from my husband. I wondered what was going to happen to my boys. I hoped Opuada had made plans for their future, because I had just spent my life as a dutiful wife, minding my business and leaving him to run his alone.

Well, it didn't take long for things to happen, as after he was laid to rest, a young man came to me, introducing himself as Opuada's lawyer. His name was Mr. Whyte. He announced that I, my sons, my sisters-in-law, and my mother-in-law were to be present for the reading of Opuada's will.

I was stunned, as I wouldn't have figured Opuada for a man who had a will. Like I said, he had a God complex. But I will say this, though. After listening to the will being read, it was obvious that Opuada had indeed been a man who put his family first, and I respected him for it even though it was during that same moment that I found out that he had a daughter and a son from another woman, who had been well taken care of by him and were also included in his will. Now I knew why he spent most of his weekends in Bonny.

Was I bitter?

Yes, I was. But I didn't fault the kids.

All Opuada's properties, the houses in Port Harcourt and in Bonny, were left in my boys' names. His business and the running of it were handed over to my first son Inye, under the tutelage of his lawyer, who was his friend Mr. Whyte, 'til he turned eighteen. I was happy that my boys were going to be taken care of. I felt a bit disappointed, as something in me wished that Opuada would have given me the task of running the business, but like I told you, he felt that my role was to remain in the kitchen.

I was happy that my greedy in-laws didn't get what they wanted, Opuada's business. He left them the family house he'd built in Bonny and a house in

Port Harcourt, but I knew they were going to die fighting over who got it and who didn't.

24ᵗʰ December, 2014.
Harmattan Season. 1.30 p.m.
Dear Diary,

For a little more than eight years, I was a widow. I had no life other than the one of being a mother and trying to take care of my children. The business their father had left for them was run down by Mr. Whyte, his so-called friend and lawyer, due to mismanagement of funds.

Thank goodness I had developed the habit of saving, meaning from Day One, all the funds I received from the business and the house rent, I saved every penny of. I never bought anything for myself. I didn't even change the cars that Opuada bought. My sisters-in-law had somehow managed to hijack the Toyota Camry we had, claiming their brother had promised them a car. Thankfully, the Honda Accord had been in the mechanic shop at the time, so I had that to myself.

You won't believe it, but this is what I have driven for the last eight years. I had to learn how to drive, as I had dismissed all the drivers after the death of my husband. With my savings, I was able to send my kids to the best of schools, and thankfully, God has blessed me with intelligent boys who are ready to go to school.

For my extended family, I reduced their stipends. Fortunately, some of my siblings had become successful, and so, the burden had lessened. We shared it all. Evenly distributed. Not just on one set of shoulders any more.

My life was a boring routine; weekdays were for school runs, 'til the last of my sons got into college.

Weekends, I stayed indoors and went to church on Sunday. A few of the church members tried to get me to become a worker there, but I refused.

During the years of my marriage to Opuada, I had grown into a hermit. I loved my own company, but eventually, it started to get to me, after more than eight years of the same routine. I was already too old for school, so I dropped that idea, but as the years passed by, I noticed that technology had improved.

We had mobile phone services in the country, and I followed the trend. Then came the Internet. I learnt what it was to be on the Web, and then, I began to get itchy again. I wanted more. I sometimes thought to myself that if I'd had the Internet when I was younger, I probably would have gone to school online, but like a person who never tried anything new, I had stuck to what I knew.

Port Harcourt that I knew as being quiet, the oil city of Nigeria, the garden city, had become over-populated. It had become dirtier, in need of more roads, and traffic was just as bad as in Lagos. Politics had become stiffer and more violent, with politicians promising and not keeping their promises. Public schools had become like grave yards with no proper facilities.

Nonetheless, I still lived in the house that we lived in when Opuada was alive, in old G.R.A, and we were still considered the *crème-de-la-crème* of society, but I never did anything to warrant that. I left the house as it was. The white chairs? Their colours had changed, turned brown even after constant washing and cleaning, but I didn't change them. I was more concerned about my son's school fees than the upholstery of our living room furniture.

When Opuada's friends' wives tried to push me to go abroad with them, I refused, letting them know that I had no money for frivolities. They usually laughed at me, but I didn't mind. I had a mission; my boys were going to get the best education.

My life was uninteresting and would have stayed that way until I met Luke. This was a chance meeting, and I could say we were destined to meet, who knows.

It was a Sunday evening, and I was at this point tired of my life and living it as society wanted it to be lived. It was the day I defied all odds and subdued my nerves as I went into my closet and put on a black pair of pencil jeans and a black, loose-fitting T-shirt that Cassandra, my *oyibo* Canadian neighbour who never took no for an answer, even though she had been unsuccessfully trying to invite me for coffee at hers for years, had given me.

Surprisingly, when I put this on, it struck me how much weight I had lost. I looked like a skinny school girl instead of a thirty-eight-year-old mother of three.

Ignoring the inquiring looks my boys gave me, I told them I was going out with my friends. I further ignored the equally curious look I got from Musa, our old reliable gateman who refused to leave us when Opuada died and was content with whatever I could pay him. With a straight face, I told him I was going out and would be back in a couple of hours.

When I got into Cassandra's house, I almost passed out in admiration—her house reflected her years of investing in it. It was a work of art and had character. Her husband, who was a Nigerian, had worked for a shipping company for years and had grown through the ranks to become the district manager, so money wasn't a problem.

When I first met her, she'd struck me as a very nice lady, but being married to Opuada, I had to be careful not to be too friendly with her so as not to arouse suspicion. She had a fantastic bookshelf with all kinds of books from different authors and genres: classics, contemporary, you name it. They were in the category of people who weren't affected by the erratic nature and shortage of electricity, as their power generator was constantly on, with a backup generator for emergency purposes.

Yes, as the years passed by, the electricity supply in Port Harcourt and the country as a whole grew worse, and so, we resorted to the constant use of generators as more dependable, alternative sources of power. When Opuada died, our constant use of a generator died with him, as I lived on a strict budget.

Thankfully, there was light today, so my ears were not disturbed by the constant generator noise. Back to Cassandra's house. Yes! It was a house with character. She had different ornaments, which she had gotten from the many countries she had travelled to. I was a bit scared. I didn't want to sit down on her chairs, so I stood all the while I waited for her.

When she came down, she was already dressed, informing me that we were going out for a drink. It took every atom in me not to decline the invite. I tried to remind her that I was a widow, and she pushed that aside, telling me that I didn't have a life and that it was time to get one, joking that it wasn't a nightclub she was taking me to, just a restaurant to have some drinks.

Well, timidly, I joined her, seated at the back seat of her Range Rover Evoque, loving the interior and reminding myself of the goodness of money. I sat quietly as we were taken to a restaurant in the new GRA, off Aba Highway Road.

The moment I saw the restaurant, I knew it was very expensive. I quickly reminded her that I didn't have the money to pay for it, and she told me not to worry, that it was a friend's birthday lunch and everything was paid for. I was a bit self-conscious about my outfit, and as though sensing it, Cassandra gave me a yellow scarf, stating that it was going to add colour to my outfit.

Looking at the scarf, as I reviewed my reflection in the rear mirror, I wrapped it on my hair like a turban. Thankfully, I was wearing the dangling gold earrings that Opuada had gotten for me when I gave birth to Inye. This made me look like an African princess. With a little lip gloss, I joined her at the entrance of the restaurant, and we both walked in.

The interior was ostentatiously furnished, and I became a bit apprehensive again. You won't blame me as this was my first time working outside my comfort zone. As though Cassandra sensed it, she took me by the hand and practically pushed me in 'til we got to the designated party area, where a long, rectangular table that could seat thirty people was arranged and sparingly occupied.

Following Cassandra's cue, I greeted the celebrant who was daintily dressed in a navy blue, figure-hugging knee-length dress. She had the perfect body, flat stomach, toned bum, narrow waist, long legs which were accentuated by her black stiletto heels. Her hair was perfectly done. I think she had one of all these new hair extensions, either Brazilian hair or Peruvian weaves. Her makeup was professionally applied, and my guess was right when I overheard her saying that she got one of the makeup artists from House of Tara makeup studio to do it. The makeup was worth it. She didn't look a day older than twenty-one.

Again, I was worried about how I looked. I saw the way her husband, whom she was taller than, was hovering around her like a parent who had just discovered that they were solely responsible for their infant child.

Leaving Cassandra to mingle, I quickly took a seat far away from the celebrant and her friends. On our way, I had asked Cassandra if I was going to pay for the bills as I had denied myself these types of frivolities for a very long time. Laughing at me, she had chided me to loosen up once again and that I shouldn't worry that for our first outing together, she was in charge of whatever bill I incurred, giving me the look like this one doesn't look like she can finish a tiny muffin.

The table quickly filled up, and drinks were served. I was tempted to have a glass of red wine, but I didn't dare. Instead, I stuck to a bottle of Coke, no ice, and followed suit as everybody went to the buffet table for the starters. As conscious as I was, I couldn't resist sampling a few of the dishes.

It was at this point I met Luke. I had seen him when he'd walked in. What I noticed was that he was very tall, one of the tallest men I had ever seen, and he was alone. Speaking to me from behind, he urged me to try the pain au chocolat and the fish pepper soup together, as although it sounded like a very weird combination, it was one he liked very much.

Laughing at him and feeling a bit adventurous, I did try it. I noticed he was observing me as I ate, especially when I almost spat out the weird combination as he tried to hide a chuckle.

Despite hating the taste, I struggled to finish it. Something else that struck me about him was the fact that he looked like an outdoorsy man. One who was used to physical activities, probably worked out a lot, too. Opuada wasn't one to care about his body and had developed a beer belly before his demise, which I minded, but as usual, had kept to myself.

My impression of Luke was that he was a no-nonsense kinda guy and possibly a flirt, too, because in my books, any Nigerian man who looked this handsome, had a bit of cash in his pocket, and moved with this circle of friends would not be lacking for women. So I quickly stopped interacting with him and looked everywhere other than where he was seated, opposite me.

Time and time again, I felt his eyes on me, making me very self-conscious. I would unconsciously wipe the side of my mouth with the serviette, thinking I mistakenly had food crumbs, but this didn't stop him. He took part in the conversations with the whole group, but I noticed he always had his gaze on me. When I accidentally spilled my drink in a bid to go and use the loo, he was the first person to respond to my silent call for help.

Quickly getting up on his feet, he picked up my purse, reassuring me not to look so forlorn as it was just a mistake. I felt something when our fingers touched, and I noticed he did, as well, because he looked at me. He had been stealing glances at me all day, but this time around, he looked hard and long at me.

Oh, his eyes, very big eyes which made you want to drown in them. I know I am a bit naive in this woman-man world, but I know when a man is interested in a woman. I could tell that he was interested in me, and I was excited. Will you blame me?

Here I was, a widow who hadn't had any male admirers since her husband had died or before... Even when I was married, I didn't get the appreciation of my husband. I don't think he ever told me I was beautiful or he liked my dress or my smile. Even when we made love, it was very mechanical. Everything was mechanical to him. Opuada had this mentality that a man's show of love was to provide for his family.

Sensing Luke's interest, I wanted it. I also knew that if I walked down this path, I wasn't going to be able to handle the explosion.

Immediately after I got back from the toilet, I mumbled some excuse to Cassandra about my kids being alone at home, and we left. I don't know why Cassandra gave in, but she promptly took me home, and I was grateful for that. For me, Luke was a door I had closed even before it had opened.

Or so I thought.

24th December, 2014.
2.30 p.m.
Dear Diary,

I am a bit exhausted, but I can't leave you hanging without completing my story.

Like I said, I was happy the door was closed, until two weeks later.

I had gone to the bank on one of those days I tried to dress up a little bit. It entailed just putting on a knee-length, African patterned dress with short sleeves. I must say that I realized as I wore the dress that I was still a tad skinny and had noted in my *To Do List* that I was going to start seeking ways to add a bit of weight, as my mother's voice rang in my head, describing how African men loathed skinny women.

So I got into my jalopy ride, and I was off to the bank, as they had all gone online and I wanted to get into online banking, as well. Mind you, this was 2012. I had procrastinated a lot about getting an ATM card until the banks said if you were withdrawing less than 50,000 Naira, you had to use your ATM card or pay through your nose withdrawing over the counter.

On my way to the bank, my jalopy gave way a few miles from my house. Very frustrated and not knowing what to do, I parked it by the roadside and opened the bonnet. Standing there, hot, upset, and frustrated, I was contemplating what to do when a black Toyota Prado parked on the side of the road. I didn't notice it until I heard a voice ask if I needed help. Immediately, goose pimples erupted on my skin. I knew who it was. The voice was one I could never forget, even in my sleep.

Turning around, I hoped he didn't notice I was blushing. That day was one of the days I wished I wore sunglasses, mainly to hide my eyes. He was a lot taller than I remembered, and I couldn't see his eyes as they were hidden beneath his sunglasses, but I could feel the intensity of his gaze.

I replied, quickly telling him that it was nothing serious as I just had to go to the bank and the car chose today to break down. He quickly pulled out his phone, called his mechanic, describing where the car was parked, by the side close to the old Mr. Biggs fast food place on Aba Road. Before I knew it, I was sitting in the passenger's seat of his car and being driven to my bank. He tried to make some conversation, but I think I was completely mute. I had lost every sense of communication. I prayed fervently that he wouldn't think me a young girl in awe of her Prince Charming. I wanted him to see me as a woman of the world, which I know I wasn't, but still.

Thinking he was going to just drop me in front of the bank and go away, imagine my shock when I heard the customer service lady flirting with someone behind me, ignoring me as she asked him if she could be of any help. As I heard his reply, I knew he was the one quickly telling the lady that he was in the bank with me.

I chuckled when I saw the look of disbelief cross her face. It felt good. You know what I mean. After my bank transaction, just outside the bank, Luke was stopped by a friend of his, who being very forward, blurted out his question, which was if I was Luke's wife and accusing him further of getting married and not inviting him.

How awkward. This was another warning sign to cap this relationship or whatever it was right that minute, but no, it felt good. I allowed myself to be lured into having breakfast at the new breakfast spot that had just opened in D-LINE, off Aba Road. It was modelled after IHOP in America, or so I was told by the server as soon we were seated.

Enjoying their pancakes, eggs, bacon, and hot chocolate, I loosened up a bit, and we talked. Now, I could see his eyes—they were the most gorgeous eyes ever. Very expressive and huge. Like I said, one could drown inside those eyes. I didn't know where the boldness came from, but it descended upon me like a pompous man who knew he had millions underneath his bed. The more questions I asked, the more I liked what I found out. He was a chef and owned a few restaurants which he ran with partners. He loved cooking and had fallen in love with it as a child. I loved this about him.

Imagine me, who was used to men who never set foot in the kitchen, and here I was, meeting a guy who knew how to cook, loved cooking, and was inviting me to his house for dinner. He had a slight accent, and when I probed further, I realized that his mother was half Ghanaian and half Irish, and his childhood had been spent back and forth in Nigeria, Ghana, and Ireland.

As I looked at him, I was still amazed that such a manly specimen would be sitting with a widow like me and not have his phone ring with his screaming wife wondering where he had run off to. When I asked him what his wife would think as he invited me for dinner, he told me he wasn't married.

It was then I asked him how old he was, and he dropped the bombshell. He was thirty-three years old, meaning I was five years older than him. I felt like I had just had a bucket of ice cold water poured over my head. This had got to stop. Another sign that he was a no-go area. I quickly told him to forgive me for being too forward, but that I didn't think that we should have any more breakfasts or anything at all together.

Even though I may have over-reacted a bit, I was adamant that it was time to get back to my car and home to my kids, stressing the kids' part so he would know that I was a woman with a lot of baggage. Not giving him an option, the breakfast ended on a sour note.

24ᵗʰ December, 2014.
4 p.m.
Dear Diary,

Hmmm, my dear, I must say this before I continue. After all my drama, I have found love. This time, I have really found love, and I now know what love really is. I am in love with Luke, and it's a bit frightening, this feeling I feel for him, even though I know that he feels it, too.

I know that my family and probably my friends won't be happy when I reveal my secret to them tomorrow, but this is how they have felt since the first time they found out about Luke. I had stood my ground then, and now, I am ready to do the same and weather the storm.

I know that he will be behind me a hundred percent. Do not get me wrong, my dear friend. Luke is not a saint. I have just realized that I have painted him as one, but he isn't. He is to me, but nobody is a saint.

I have been with him for a short period of time, which a few of my friends have let slip out the bag. I find that sometimes, he can be very forgetful. It makes my emotions go up and down, but I have to relax about this. He also writes down a lot of things. I like to write, as well, but he does that a lot more than me. I had teased him a few days ago that he must be an aspiring writer. He had looked at me funny, not in a weird way but like he wanted to say something and would have if we hadn't been interrupted.

I know you still want the juicy part of the story, so let me continue. I just wanted to put out the disclaimer before we moved any further.

Yes, finding out that I was older than him by five years was such a big deal for me. With all the odds that were against me, I thought it would never work.

Number One—I am a widow, and you know widows are supposed to remain nuns for the rest of their lives, although it is a bit different with widowers, as everyone keeps on telling the man that he should find a wife as he cannot be alone for too long. But nobody ever thinks of the fact that women have feelings, as well. The woman, who is me in this instance, was to remain a log of wood. Unresponsive, undisturbed by any sexual desires which were deemed carnal for a good woman. But who told them that?

Being with Luke had evoked feelings I had never expected that I could ever feel.

With Opuada, like I said earlier, lovemaking was mechanical. I never understood or knew what an orgasm meant until I met Luke.

Okay, slow down. I didn't immediately jump into bed with him, no way. In fact, he took it very slow with me. He always told me that he would wait for me. He wanted to marry me from the first time we met, he said. I was the one who couldn't wait any longer. I know some people may see me as a lustful, wanton woman, but do they understand?

Have they ever felt such strong chemistry for someone?

With Luke, I felt everything. I lusted after him. I was in love with him. I desired him. I wanted him to make sweet love to me constantly. One day after an awesome love making bout, he whispered in my ear when he thought I might have drifted to sleep that he was glad he hadn't forgotten how to give me pleasure.

I wanted to respond back saying, "so long as you do not forget my name and how to satisfy me, I am very fine," but I let him be in his world, because he really did love me.

I wanted him to take me to our world, a world which was older than our forefathers' generations. A world only experienced by a man and woman in love, and he absolutely did.

I tried my best to guard this part of my heart and feelings. I tried not to explore it, but Luke was persistent. I couldn't understand what a man like him saw in a woman like me. He said he loved my hair. I always loathed my hair. It was so full, very long, and very uncooperative, so I always packed it up under a wig.

Now, because of Luke, I learnt to wear my hair out. It is still kinky, uncooperative, and very full, but I must admit it gave me somewhat of a wild, daring look which I love.

He said he loved my figure. I had always considered my body a disappointment because I was flat-bummed and small-chested even after having kids. When I was younger, I was nicknamed *oyibo*, and I detested it.

But Luke loved everything about me. He said that with him being big, he was attracted to me as a petite lady. He loved my small round breasts as they disappeared inside his big palms when he stroked my nipples to submission. He loved my little round bottom and urged me to dress complimenting my body, and so I did. If you ask me, I would say Luke knew who I was. I just had it hidden for so long that I had forgotten.

I have become more daring, so much so that I now wear figure-hugging dresses, skinny jeans, and slinky and skinny tops. I even risked wearing shorts once when Luke and I went for a walk on the beach. I must say, that day, all through the drive, Luke couldn't keep his hands off me. If I was a meal, I am sure he would have eaten me and wanted more.

I was afraid, because, look at me, I am an older woman with grown kids, and in my head and by society's standards, I was considered old cargo, but he told me he didn't see me that way. Although to be honest, he understood a bit of what I was saying as he had a son, too. Even when I pushed him away from me, telling him that we couldn't work, everything from me being older than him to me having kids and being a widow, not considered fresh goods by society, he wouldn't listen to me.

He came back after one week. We couldn't stay apart longer than that.

24th December, 2014.
9 p.m.
Dear Diary,

It's bed time, and my birthday is tomorrow. I can't wait, because like I told you, I am going to reveal my secret to everyone, all my guests. Right now, I do not care what is going to happen as I have already thought about everything.

I know you may be worried for me, but I have thought this thing through, and I know that this is the best decision I have ever made. In fact, this is the first decision I have ever made for myself. All my life, I have lived for other people, for my parents, for my siblings, for my late husband, and for my children. Tomorrow will begin a journey where I live my life for myself, and to think that I had pushed Luke away for so long.

I had told Luke to leave me alone, and he did for about a week, but we both couldn't stay apart from each other. One Sunday, I saw him in my house. Musa, the gate man, called me saying one *Oga* wanted to see me. Thinking it must be one of Opuada's relations, I told him to let the person in.

Imagine my shock when I saw Luke walk in. Since we started dating, it had been a rule that he was never to come to my house. We always met somewhere else. He never liked it, as he wanted to show me off to the whole world. Time and time again, I tried to make him understand that being a man, his world was a whole lot different from mine. People won't judge him, but they will not hesitate to judge me.

Well, he didn't listen, and he came to my house. This was the first time my boys saw him; they were home for the holidays then. Of course, Inye was very suspicious of him, but my other boys were smitten. They kept asking me where I met this basketball player with a strange accent. I told them he was just my friend, and when Inye wanted to probe further, I shut him up.

Well, when Luke came back, I knew that I had to choose to be with him, giving all of myself or not being with him at all. I chose being with him. He was very happy, and he took me to meet his family. I was scared to death that I wouldn't be accepted, but his mother, although apprehensive at first, warmed up to me. I like to think it was the Irish and Ghanaian blood that ran through her veins that was talking. She seemed to sympathize with me when she learnt I had married so early, as she oversaw a Non-Governmental Organization which was set up to eradicate child bride practices and so, one could say that made her more responsive to me and my background.

The main hurdle was my in-laws and my family. My in-laws already saw me as a gold digger and had never liked me even though I had always done everything I could to please them. They would come and stay in my house when Opuada was alive, for months on end, and I would feed and accommodate them with all their outrageous demands, from being only occasional vegetarians to eating certain foods that could only be found in the most luxurious grocery stores in Port Harcourt.

So, I wasn't surprised when they labelled me a prostitute and the one who'd killed their brother. They called me a witch and said that I was going to marry a man who would finish their brother's money. Imagine their shock when they found out who I was going to get married to.

Apparently, Luke's family name carried weight in Port Harcourt and beyond, and they all knew that he was filthy rich. They called me a callous woman and one who didn't deserve children. I listened to all they said and then thanked them and walked away. I was happy at this point that my sons were old enough to take care of themselves. I was happy, as well, that Luke was at my side staring at them menacingly and daring anybody to come close to laying a finger on me. I knew deep down that Opuada's sisters were jealous, because they had nothing and had never aspired to be any better.

The next stop was my parents'. I travelled to Bonny to inform them. Well, I can tell you that it wasn't pleasant, as well. As my father chased me away from his house, claiming that I had disgraced him, he asked me if I knew any women who had kids and followed men up and down. My dad wasn't thinking straight because his sister apparently had kids from different men.

The last people I told, and this, I dragged for as long as I could, were my kids. Of course, Inye was mad. He didn't call me a prostitute directly but did indirectly; he was very hard on me and started blackmailing me emotionally. He told me that if I went ahead and married Luke, he was never going to speak to me again and that he was going to instruct his brothers to do the same. I would have thought that with all the sacrifices I had made for him, he would at least be by my side. I lived for my children. Right now, Inye has graduated from a very prestigious university in America and was going straight for his Masters' degree.

Who did he think paid for it? Me.

Yes, he can say it was his father's money, but if it hadn't been managed properly, how would he have had a quality education? My last two boys called me after two weeks of tormenting me with their silence. Abel, the ever logical one, asked me if I loved Luke, and when I replied that I did, he said then I should follow my heart, and something that he never liked to admit was that he had never seen me this happy as I was with Luke. I thanked him, cried with him, and cyber-hugged him.

The relationship was still not easy. I noticed the way people turned and looked at us whenever we went out. Luke was physically expressive about his love, and I was not. In a town where married people hardly took leisure walks together for instance, Luke would do that. He would kiss me in public without any care in the world. He would never walk with me by his side without holding my hand, firmly.

Anyway, it's time to get to bed, as tomorrow is the big day. Tomorrow is the day I turn forty, and it is the day I reveal my secret.

25th December, 2014.
Party in Progress. 2 p.m.
Dear Diary,
Today, I tell my family and my friends that I will be leaving Nigeria. I am moving abroad. Luke and I are going to live somewhere. Where, exactly, we haven't figured out yet, but right now, we are on the next flight to America. We will go on road trips around the United States and then fly to Europe, discovering it, and after that, we may probably settle somewhere in South East Asia, as Luke and some of his partners are opening an office there. They more or less want to establish their roots in Asia.

Every time I think of our life ahead, I think of how stupid I was to even suggest such a thing as ending this relationship. Advising Luke to leave me. I shouldn't have let myself go through such heartbreak even though it wasn't for a long period of time. I will also never forget his words to me when we got back together. He said, "Babe, I might forget a lot of things, but don't ever tell me to leave you alone. That, I couldn't forget. It was pure torture listening to you say those words."

That had made me very emotional, no surprise there. As you can tell, we've decided to put that aside and move on in our relationship.

Did I tell you that Luke is a successful business man as well as a successful chef? No, I don't think so. Well, he is. And with the growth of information technology which fascinates him, Asia may just be a very good base to pitch their tent with all the new apps and gadgets he has developed.

For me, I think I have a whole new world to explore. I am going back to school. And no, I am not going to study Theatre Arts. I am probably going to do something in creative writing. I think I want to be a travel writer, share a few experiences of my travels. I am a bit wary about this new journey partly because I can see the disbelief, shock, condemnation, envy, spite, and the discouragement in the eyes of my friends and family. Everyone told me that I was crazy when I told them that I had decided to move away.

My in-laws were the loudest as I quickly handed them the keys to the house. They have always wanted what was Opuada's, and I told them it was now theirs, they could have it, and after all, I had gotten a good lawyer and made sure that the ten apartments that Opuada had left for the boys stayed with them.

When they asked what would happen with my boys, I told them they will be with me. Right now, they are aged twenty-two, twenty-one, and twenty, all grown and independent, and so, it is time to live my life.

When my family and friends expressed their displeasure, holding Luke's hands in mine, I urged him not to say a word, even though it was killing him to remain silent. I laughed at them within me; they really did not know how much I have changed. They did not know that I was no longer the same person. They did not know that I no longer think about what they say or not.

Right now, it is time to live my life. I look up at Luke, and I smile. I can see the love in his eyes for me. I still can't believe that he loves me. His height and physical magnificence always amaze me. I wonder if I will ever get used to it.

As I write this, I chuckle, and I am a bit shy, but I will say this, anyway. I remember when we first made love; I was so worried about his height and me being very small. He, on the other hand, was so worried about hurting me because he knew that after Opuada, I hadn't been with any man.

I remember the way I felt when I saw his body. I had a strange tingling within my legs, which I later understood was desire. I was scared and waited for him in apprehension. It was a bit awkward for a man who was worldly, and I found it amusing that he wasn't so confident with me at first. It took me a while to relax with him, too.

It was almost a world war to strip in front of him, and I was grateful I had remembered to shave the previous night. I had anticipated this, but at the same time, I was nervous, thoughts like *what if I can't satisfy him* kept bugging me, or if my body was undesirable. You won't blame me, as I have previously said, with Opuada, it was mechanical.

With Luke, it was different. It was painful the first time, like losing my virginity all over again, but then, Luke engaged me through a journey of self-discovery as he took his time daily, slowing exploring my body, learning what I liked and what pleased and excited me.

Amazingly, I wouldn't have thought that I could be so responsive any time he touched me or as much as glanced at me. My dear, I said he did things that even I didn't believe could happen in lovemaking. What he did to me, I used to think was a sin, but if it is a sin, I think I am ready to live with it for the rest of my life because he took me to Heaven and back.

Ha! This Luke, my dear Luke. The only man who can make me think wild things.

Where didn't we make love? We did it everywhere. After the daily lessons of discovering that I, as a woman, had sexual desires, I was like a bird that had been released from the cage into the wild, to soar, and soar I did.

We made love everywhere: on top of the car, under the moon and stars, in the swimming pool, on the kitchen counter top, in the bathtub, standing, sitting, crawling. *Hmmmm,* my dear, I said I was like a wild bird. I still am like a wild bird and can't get enough of him.

Well, this is my reality. I am in love with a younger guy, and I am not ashamed to say it.

Remember, I told you he had a son. Well, when we are through with our tour, he will come to live with us, same with my boys as a family.

Will we have kids together?

Right now, I suspect I am even pregnant as my period is a couple of days late, but I have to be sure before I announce it, and if it is true, I will be happy, even though this will change our whole plan. We will still go to America because we leave tonight, anyway, but I doubt we will do the European tour 'til after the baby is born. It will be nice to see what our kid will look like. Luke will love it, and I think he will be the best father in the world.

I am in love. I know you are tired of hearing me confess my love, but I can't fail to repeat it. Oh, and yes, Luke and I have to thank Cassandra for inadvertently orchestrating our meeting. If she hadn't dragged me for her friend's party, I may never have met him.

I can hear him calling me now, so it's time to go. Our flight is at about eleven p.m. tonight, and I fly business class, which I'm eagerly anticipating. This is going to be my first experience flying so. I am a bit nervous, but Luke says I shouldn't worry. It will be all right.

It's time to say good bye. You have been such a good and understanding friend. I do not know when we will get the opportunity to talk again, who knows, but I will keep in touch. All I say is this: just pray for me that our love grows stronger and stronger, because I know that Luke is the man I want to spend the rest of my life with.

25th December, 2014.

10 p.m.

We have boarded; I am on the plane. For starters, I didn't know planes were this huge. Business class is fantastic! Already, I have been served a glass of red wine, and champagne is on the way. I know I will be drunk by the time we get to our destination, but I am as excited as a kid in a candy store and can't believe this is my life. I know you may think that this is all make-believe and it can only happen in movies or books, but believe me, this is my life, and it is only going to get better.

Epilogue

Dear Diary,

This will be my last entry in a long while. I do not know when I will be back, but that's something I will decide. I am excited about my trip with Luke, as you know—I have made up my mind to enjoy every bit of this journey as one never knows what life brings.

Having said that, I have stared at Luke a million times, when he is snoring lightly besides me, most times after several rounds of sweet love making, and I wonder if my present situation is real.

Most people might think me a fool to love again and this time be different in the way I love.

Most people might think me stupid to love like a teenage girl, experiencing a feeling supernaturally unexplainable, and I do not blame them. I have painted Luke as the perfect man, my knight in shining armour. He is indeed one that makes no mistakes, but like everyone, he is not perfect. Honestly, we've had our fair share of arguments, and I am even shocked at how childish these have been.

The small voice sometimes taunts me that this would soon end and I would be back to rock bottom with nothing to fall back on. Sometimes, I heed this voice, and I act out in fear that everything would be gone soon.

But then, Luke reminds me that life usually is what you make of it. He reminds me that he, too, is afraid and not sure about himself or our lives together, but he is ready to see this through. I must have repeated myself a million times, but I, too, am ready to see this through.

I have buckled up, and it's time to say good bye. Please remember me in your prayers. Not that I am spiritual, but it wouldn't hurt to know that you all care about me and my relationship.

Pray that this would be my happily ever after, as I know deep down in my heart it is.

Pray that mine and Luke's bond strengthens as we grow closer.

Pray that tragedy doesn't befall us, and above all, I pray that you, too, find the love of your life at some point of your existence as I have.

Signed,

Ere

223 Bonny Street
by
FIRI KAMSON

BLURB

Set in the south-east of Nigeria, 223, Bonny Street is a story about surviving loss, finding your identity, and making connections.

After an accident, waking up in another person's body seems like a dream until Ikenna realizes that he is faced with the stark reality of Nkechi's life, the woman whose body he occupies. He thus experiences the pain and joy, the strength and sacrifices of a woman.

The two of them make a connection beyond the physical, but matters of the heart are delicate. When secrets from the past are revealed, will their connection be strong enough to survive?

PROLOGUE

The rain was pouring non-stop, the weather ripe for lovers, but the atmosphere wasn't one for lovemaking, as the people of Biafra were at war with the Nigerians, and the Biafrans were quite determined to win.

Finding a safe shelter was as difficult as forcing a camel through the eye of a needle. Fathers, mothers, sisters, and brothers were ready to protect themselves, taking cover as soon as the sirens went off, to avoid the bullets from the foot soldiers. Confusion swirled in the air as families trooped in with their wounded, seeking help, refuge, and food.

It had been a busy day for Data and her family at the vicarage, the result of the bomb blast in Nsukka, and now, everyone knew the worst had come. Nsukka, the heart of Enugu state, was a very peaceful and quiet town, excellent for academics. A university town home to one of the most prestigious tertiary schools in the country at the time, The University of Nsukka, everything revolved around this place.

Data remembered the peaceful days when her father would entertain a few of the foreign lecturers in the vicarage, and on those days, he would bring out a bottle of red wine which he had hidden carefully, away from prying eyes.

Now, all that was long gone with the onset of the war. Farmers, who prided themselves on the growth and fortunes their crops brought them during the harvest period, had lost everything.

Data sensed she had to increase her ability to multitask as she looked around, and after doing a rough estimation in her head, the queue didn't seem to have shortened.

Observing a commotion close to the door, she looked up from where she was assisting the newborn babies, swaddling them in blankets that weren't as dirty as the wrappers on their mothers' bodies to keep them warm whilst wondering to herself how women could find the time to have sex with their husbands in wartime.

Glancing up, she noticed the arrival of a fresh batch of people, including a young man who couldn't be more than twenty years old, carrying a woman covered in blood. As she listened, the young man screamed in Igbo that someone should please help his mother, as she was the only family he had left.

Quickly leaving instructions with the mother she was with on how to properly breastfeed her child, Data stood up. She straightened her already faded and wrinkled skirt to at least cover her knees and ran to the door at the same time as her father, the priest.

"Data, bring out the first aid kit from my office," he called.

She ran towards his office at the vicarage.

He was the Anglican priest of the church, and this position had afforded them a few privileges since the war had begun, as a lot of the aid gotten from the foreign aid workers was brought to the church. Data usually helped her father with the distribution, and this singular act had helped in preventing her, her family, and anybody who took shelter with them from the deadly enemy. An enemy worse than war itself, the dreaded kwashiorkor.

This was why it was very important for them, especially her father, to stay safe at all times. Picking up the first aid box, she looked around his office for the first time since they'd gotten here.

It looked like his old office, with the same sort of décor, and it served as his sanctuary as well as the previous one had. Even though it wasn't the same room, it still reminded her of the days she would come into his office to see him, and the various bits of advice she would receive from him while picking up one of his philosophy books to read. Then, when she got bored, she would sneak in a romance novel, hiding the cover from her mother's inquisitive eyes with an old newspaper.

War really changed things. How could she have forgotten so quickly how she would just come to his office and have coffee and cookies with her father, the sweet tooth, while he would tell her stories about his childhood, which always fascinated her?

Sighing, she exited the room quickly and ran to the church door. Noticing that her mother had already prepared a makeshift bed, she wasn't surprised that the woman had taken over quickly. Her mother was a trained nurse, known by everyone as Nurse Bristol, and she knew how to work very well under pressure.

Forcibly bringing her mind back to the present, Data cut open what remained of the lady's clothes. It was difficult to tell where she had been wounded as her whole body was covered in blood. Data almost vomited as, no matter how many times she had seen bloodied bodies, she still always had the urge to vomit whenever she saw one. This was why she had not followed her mother's footsteps to become a nurse. She instead took after her father, a teacher.

Covering her mouth with her handkerchief, she stayed by her mother's side, ready to give her whatever she needed for the emergency operation sure to follow. She watched her mother as she rapidly cleaned the blood off the woman.

Noticing that she had a gunshot wound by the side of her stomach, Data stopped herself from gagging once again. Listening to her mother as she explained to the lady in Igbo that she was going to try and extricate the bullet and stop the bleeding, she hoped the lady had a high threshold for pain.

Without waiting for her mother's cue, she had already opened the first aid box, and bringing out a bottle, she opened it, pouring some *kai kai* into the cover, then she handed it to her mother. Since they weren't in a proper hospital and there wasn't anything to sterilize wounds with, her mother had converted her father's prized native gin, which everyone called *kai kai* and reserved for the village elders' visits, to a sterilizer. A pair of scissors instead of a surgical knife was employed, as they had to make use of what they had.

Following instructions, she held the woman's legs down while the son held her hands and her father stood by her side, talking in a soothing voice to the lady, telling her things that Data felt were not necessary, but apparently, her father thought they would help distract her from the pain.

The lady struggled and screamed as soon as her mother poured the *kai kai* on her skin, telling her to bravely bear the sting as it was for her own good. Her mother then stuck the knife into the woman's stomach as she meticulously dug out the bullet, amidst all the screaming and trying to get the lady to lie still. Data looked at the son and watched as tears ran down his face while he promised her he wasn't going to leave her alone and that he was always going to be with her.

Passing a threaded needle to her mother, Data watched again as she sewed up the wound after treating it. Cleaning it up, she told the lady that she would just have to pray to heal properly and quickly, and that hopefully, they would be able to stay in the vicarage without having to run for their lives a little longer, as the war had gotten even more intense.

Giving her one of her herbal concoctions to drink, her mother instructed the lady to rest, and, promising her everything would be all right by God's grace, she left. Bringing forward a makeshift stool for the son, Data told him to sit down, as his mother was dozing off.

"I don't want her to die. She is all I have got left," he wailed.

"I have seen a lot during this war, and I can see that your mother is very strong. Don't worry, she seems like a fighter, and she will surely fight 'til the end." Placing a hand on his shoulder, she consoled as she fought the turmoil inside her.

"I hope I can stay as positive as you because this war has taken everything from us. I have lost everyone. My father, my two older brothers who were conscripted into the army, everybody. I am all she has, and she is all I have." He sighed.

Speechless, and with nothing else to do, Data walked away hoping that his mother would live. The war had gone on for so long now and had started taking a toll on all of them. She was like her father in the sense that she didn't want war; all her father wanted was peace. Nicknamed a man of peace, he was the one everybody ran to when they had problems in Nsukka, Port Harcourt, and Bonny.

It was her father who calmed the storm and solved the problem when Mr. Godspower was furious because his sons had poured sand into the generator and caused it to break down the day he'd brought his new wife home. In all his wisdom, he was able to pacify both sides and end the argument amicably. So, her father hated the war and sufferings of any kind. He had tried to see if he could talk to Lieutenant-Colonel Chukwuemeka Odumegwu Ojukwu, the then-military governor of Eastern Nigeria and his allies, before the war began.

At the time, she had laughed to herself and tried to dissuade him from such ventures, but he'd persisted, albeit unsuccessfully. He felt that if only he could have seen the lieutenant and his cronies, the war wouldn't have begun, although Data thought otherwise.

The Igbo community had lamented a lot about being marginalized. They complained about everything going to the *Yorubas* and the *Hausas* and being left with nothing. They talked about the discrimination they faced in the workplace, especially in the government agencies and parastatals. They also talked about their brothers and family members dying one by one in the North at the hands of their neighbors who felt they had come to harvest their land, and nothing was done to protect them.

Being a new teacher in the Federal government girls' school in Enugu, which was the capital of Nsukka, the discrimination was all the teachers talked about in staff meetings and during lunch breaks. No matter what topic they began discussing, it all got back to the injustice the Igbo people received. Data would never forget the day of the incident with Mrs.

Nwosu, the English teacher with a very thick Igbo accent who was very difficult to understand.

Mrs. Nwosu had the habit of only speaking English when she was teaching and switched to Igbo the moment she was out of the classroom. Thankfully, living in Nsukka, Data had learnt to understand and speak fluent Igbo. So, that fateful day, she had been about to get her things and go back home, exhausted and in need of some rest, when she'd met Mrs. Nwosu by the door.

Courtesy had demanded that she chatted a little bit with her, but little did she know she was opening a can of worms as Mrs. Nwosu began her sermon. Telling her how she would have been a lecturer in the University of Ibadan, a professor in English, but she had been denied the opportunity because she wasn't a Yoruba woman.

According to her, she was overqualified for the role, but because she was Igbo, the job was not given to her. She lamented about how she could not wait to live in the new country called The Republic of Biafra.

Data had tried to explain to her the implications of becoming a separate country, to no avail. After a lot of persuasion, she had decided to listen to the lieutenant's speech. The lieutenant must have been her first crush; she couldn't take her eyes off him. She had never seen anybody who could speak so eloquently and passionately about a cause.

When the speech was over, she still hadn't been in support of the war, but she couldn't deny the fact that there seemed to be no other end. All in all, she knew that the war was going to bring a lot of heartbreak, and it had. Looking around the church sanctuary, she almost cried. This was her father's holy place; it was always kept clean and devoid of anything filthy. Now, it served as a makeshift hospital, with an emergency room, kitchen, everything.

Her mother, her father, and she assumed the varied roles of priests, doctors, and nutritionists.

"Please, I need you to go and get me *Ufuba,* so I can make some soup for everybody. At least, it will be able to keep the body strong for a few days 'til the next supply comes in," her mother spoke as she handed her a black nylon bag. "Try to get as much as you can", she added as she looked around. "You can see that we now have so many mouths to feed, and I cannot just neglect them no matter how many they are," she finished sadly.

"Don't worry, *sister,* I will try my best," Data assured her mother, and taking the bag, she walked away.

Nurse Bristol watched her daughter as she walked out of the sanctuary and sighed. Normally, she would have tried to remind her to call her mummy instead of sister, but right now, she didn't have the capacity to do any of that. The main focus was staying alive and staying strong 'til the war ended. She knew her daughter didn't do it on purpose—it was a name she'd picked up from all her numerous sisters' children whom she'd had to take care of as their fathers had abandoned them. They all called her sister, as a sign of respect, so when Data was born, she automatically followed suit. She sighed again and hoped that her daughter would come back safely as always. She knew she couldn't bear it if she lost Data.

Walking away, Data couldn't take her mind off their living conditions. It wasn't that they were extremely rich before the war, but it was glaring what war could do to the people, a community, and a tribe. Before the war, who would have thought of using

Ufuba leaves, or cassava leaves as the Catholic Irish nuns called it, in making soup? Her father who never joked with his food always ate *Garri* and *Ukazi* soup everyday; it was his favorite meal, and he loved it. But sadly, since the war broke out, things one had taken for granted all disappeared, and she had to search for the cassava leaves in the forest.

As soon as the war began, the Nigerian government had put up a blockade, and everything had been shut down. There wasn't any access by air or sea, so this caused a lot of starvation. Her father had initially wanted to move back to Port Harcourt. He said he was tired of living in the eastern part of Nigeria and wanted to be nearer his home town, Bonny Island, but Data sensed that he had hesitated a bit longer because she had just been accepted as a History teacher in Queen's School Enugu, which was one of the best federal government schools in Nigeria at the time.

Who knows, maybe life might have been easier in Port Harcourt, and she wished her father had moved back there because Nsukka, which previously seemed to be one of the safest towns, was one of the first to fall to the Nigerian armed forces, and like chickens fighting for their survival, everybody ran for safety.

The war had lasted almost a year, and she had seen people die of starvation and kwashiorkor. She had seen people leave their older loved ones behind to die because they were too weak to keep running. She knew people ate all sort of creepy creatures, but had never imagined it would happen close to home until the war broke out. Due to the famine, she had seen people eat lizards, rats, and all sorts of unsavory things just to stay fed and have the strength to run whenever the bombing raids began. And although her family hadn't gotten to that point, they had discovered the use of cassava leaves.

The cassava leaves made the soups taste a bit like a sweet and sour sauce, which she detested as it gave her a feeling of cooked rice mixed with sugar syrup, but she had no choice as food was now a luxury, and since it had been confirmed that it helped keep kwashiorkor at bay, she had no choice.

Looking around, she realized it wasn't even midday yet. The sun was still blazing hot, and the roads were deserted, with decaying dead bodies littered around. She had gotten used to the smell of decomposing bodies, to the point where she didn't have to stop breathing anytime she perceived the offensive smell.

The things that the war brought were unimaginable. Circumstances that up until a few months prior had felt like abomination were now nothing but an everyday occurrence.

Suddenly feeling funny under her feet, she looked down. Realizing that her slipper strap had snapped, she took her shoes off and picked them up to see if there could be anything done to reduce the damage. After realizing that there wasn't any hope for the slippers, she threw them away, right into the bush without breaking her steps as she marched purposefully on, in her bare feet.

Spotting a huge pile of the cassava leaves, she quickly picked up as much as the bag could carry, squeezing a lot in, and satisfied that it was sufficient to last a while, she decided to follow the hidden path in the bushes, as being on the road even though it was very sunny was very lonely, leaving one vulnerable to enemy attack.

Picking up a small branch from a fallen tree, she converted it to a walking stick, and using it to clear the path, she quickened her steps. It felt just like yesterday when the war broke out and her parents ran from Nsukka to come and pick her up from school in Enugu, only a few months after she had moved into the staff quarters. Her journey up 'til date sounded more like a script for a Nigerian movie, but it certainly was her reality, which she still couldn't comprehend.

Her father and mother had arrived in a red Passat with all the stuff they could carry, urging her to come along with them. She remembered she didn't have the luxury to take anything apart from the clothes she had on her back as her mother urged her to waste no second, time being of the essence if they were to stay safe. They had spent the night in her father's friend's house, all of them sleeping with one eye open and ears cocked towards the doors in case they heard any incoming air strikes.

Very early the next day, they had quickly gotten up, and without so much as brushing their teeth, they had jumped into the car and taken off again. Thinking back, she realized how much she had taken for granted before the war began, such as the daily ritual of brushing one's teeth and taking a bath—brushing her teeth at least three times a day was a weird routine of hers.

The morning they'd left her father's friend's house, there hadn't been any time to remember to brush or take a shower, as the ultimate goal had been staying alive. She'd spent the whole day with her heart in her mouth, hoping and praying that they weren't caught, and she would never forget the relief, although temporary, that her family had felt when they'd finally gotten to her Auntie Rose's house, her mother's older sister in Aba, who was also a teacher.

Like everything that happened during war time, one never stayed in a place for a long time, and so, they'd continued running. It was a lot easier to do so in the red Passat, but during wars, nothing good lasted forever. So, finally, her father had lost the car when they'd gotten to Umuahia, which was the town in Abia state, where they presently were. Losing the red Passat had been a good thing and a bad thing at the same time, as with the Passat, it had been easier to 'run' several kilometers an hour, but because of its colour, it had also been very easy to spot, which had made them an easy target for the soldiers.

Data felt that the vicarage which had now been converted into a safe haven for everybody, irrespective of tribe or religion, served as a blessing and a curse for them. Since her father insisted on wearing his collar everywhere he went, he was immediately recognized as a priest. Automatically, people begged him for help, and since he was a man with a giving heart, he never turned down the opportunity to help anybody in need, and so, he was constantly helping. Even when he was tired, he made sure he tried his best.

When they finally lost the Passat and they were trying to get to the vicarage in Umuahia from Aba, her little cousin, Iprinye, who was about six years old at the time the war broke out, was exhausted and couldn't continue any more. She had practically fainted, and quickly containing the situation, her father had instructed her mother to calm Iprinye's mother down because she had already started screaming hysterically that she was losing her child to the war.

Swiftly bringing out the bottle of water he had wrapped under his cassock, he had made her drink to her heart's content, and then, picking her up, he had carried her on his back and tied his cassock round his waist firmly, making it impossible for her to fall. As soon as he was sure it was fastened, he'd looked at everyone, making sure they were complete as he did a head count.

Discovering some more cassava leaves on her way, Data picked them up, and holding them in her left hand, she mused to herself that it wasn't all bad as there were good things discovered during the war. Even if it was things like the cooperation between the Catholic priests, Anglican priests, volunteers, and aid workers—they worked together in distributing the aid that was smuggled in, without any inhibitions.

Data hated most of what they brought in, but she forced herself to eat it as it helped people stay alive and somewhat healthy during the war. Her worst was something called *formula two*—it was concentrated protein and most needed for survival during the war. She could never forget how her father tried to give everybody something no matter how little, and people queued up in lines so long that they seemed never to end. A rare commodity like salt was hidden gold and cherished like diamonds.

Suddenly hearing footsteps belonging to someone else, she turned around, and whilst she did not see anybody, she couldn't overlook the feeling that someone was following her. Turning back to look again, she sensed immediate danger and started running.

Only then did she hear the footsteps chasing after her closely. Increasing her speed and running as fast as her legs could take her, she heard a voice commanding her to stop, and, trembling, she obeyed. She initially contemplated not stopping, but her father had warned her sternly that when she heard that expression 'stop, or I will shoot,' she should always obey. And obey, she did. Trying to get her legs to stop trembling, she stood still as she waited.

"Will you turn around immediately?" the voiced commanded.

Wasting no time, Data turned around, ignoring the bushes that swept all over her legs, causing them to itch. Looking at the soldier, she thought to herself that he appeared so young and couldn't be older than his early thirties.

"Please, I do not want any trouble. I am just looking for something to eat," she replied carefully.

From his accent and uniform, she could tell that he was a Nigerian soldier, not a Biafran.

"Shut up," he screamed.

Putting her trembling hands on her mouth, Data tried to stay entirely still. Just then, she heard another footstep behind her, and her heart sank as she turned. The expression on the soldier's face said it all.

Listening as instructions were given to the soldiers, she watched as he pointed his gun at her. Looking around her, she searched for an escape route. She thought of running into the forest, but she wasn't sure if there were more Nigerian soldiers lurking in the bushes. The other option was running onto the main roads, but she was going to be an easy target for the soldier and be brought to her knees before she knew it.

Turning around as she sought an exit, anything to just get out of this situation, a hand twice the size of hers grabbed her and threw her on the ground into the bushes. Screaming, she pleaded with her captor, one of the tallest men she had ever seen. She begged him, told him she would do anything if he would just release her. All her words fell on deaf ears as he barked out orders to the junior soldier, instructing him to make sure nobody disturbed him.

When he ripped her dress that had undergone numerous washings, causing it to tear apart like a slice of bread, Data started fighting back. She kicked and pushed and screamed, to no avail, as it was as though the more she screamed and fought, the more sexually aroused her attacker became. Trying to run away and almost succeeding when he stood up to unzip his trousers earned her several blows on the face. Using her hands as a shield, Data wished she could just die, as her skull couldn't take any more. She just wanted to leave this world, but death was far away.

Screaming at her and calling her *ashawo*, the devil's incarnate sent to tempt him, the soldier ripped off what remained of her dress with his right hand. While he held both her hands above her head with the left as he forced himself inside her, Data felt like he had torn her whole body in two.

With her screaming at the top of her voice at the excruciating pain, the soldier cursed her while he rammed into her faster and faster, almost to the beat of her screams. Finally, after grunting at the top of his voice like an animal in heat, he quickly stood up and spat at her. Turning towards the junior solider, he left instructions that this was to be a secret or else he was never going to see another day, and then, he walked away.

One thing was sure, Data would never forget this day; the tears ran down her face as she felt the liquid pour out from between her legs. Attempting to stand up, she couldn't stop her limbs from trembling. After her second futile attempt, she watched helplessly as the junior soldier picked her up and leaned her against the side of the tree. Suddenly finding the strength to move, she limped away to hide behind the tree.

Picking up her torn dress, and without looking at her, he stretched out his hands. "Please leave now before anything else happens to you," he said.

"Nothing can ever be worse than this," she replied.

Dragging her things from the soldier, however, she ran for her dear life, as fast as her feet could carry her. She ran all the way home, falling at intervals, but she didn't care. All she wanted to do was be somewhere safe.

***

After almost three years of fighting the Biafran war, the Biafrans surrendered, and the war was eventually declared over. But then, with the end of the war came more troubles.

Determined to go back to his home state, Mr. Omoni Bristol succeeded in getting a lorry to convey people who wanted to go back to their states of origin. So Data joined her parents, aunties, and uncles as they all got into the lorry. Her father's dream had come to pass—they had survived the war, the running, and all the hunger, and now, it was time to go home.

Everybody smiled. Her mother was grateful a new beginning had come. This feeling was strange to Data. It had been months since she'd felt anything positive. She could never recount to anybody what had happened to her that fateful day, but she knew they all knew. She'd seen it in their faces and on their expressions when they'd seen her stagger into the mission house.

She would never forget the way her mother had screamed and fallen to her knees as she'd wailed and cried and screamed hysterically. Her father, ever the peacemaker, had run towards her, and carrying her like a little baby, he'd cleaned her up as best as he could while the tears rolled down from his eyes.

It had taken her months before she could even say a word. On several occasions, she had been literally dragged under the table in protection from shootings from the Nigerian ground soldiers. She didn't care if she lived or died. She had even contemplated suicide, but had been too much of a coward to see it through.

Walking into the house, she listened as her father called everybody together into the little parlor, instructing all of them to hold hands while he prayed.

He prayed, thanking his maker that he had finally gotten home, to his house, 223, Bonny Street. He blessed it and declared it a blessing to them. He prayed, thanking his cousin, Gogo, and his wife, Blessing, who had saved the house during the war. They had chased away who they'd found living there, announcing publicly that the house belonged to their brother.

223, Bonny Street was significant to him because it was where he could finally call home. Her father was happy, and as he prayed, he blessed everyone. Saying the grace, he did a head count as usual, and satisfied that they were all the complete number of forty-two, he dismissed everyone.

That night, Data slept in the room with her parents. She had opted to sleep on the floor while her parents slept on the bed, but they had declined, insisting that she slept on the bed.

As she laid down on her back, she looked at her protruding stomach. She felt the child moving, and she cried again. One part of her wanted to hate the child for all it represented and stood for while another part of her wanted to love it, as it was innocent.

"Data, will you eat something?" Nurse Bristol asked her daughter.

"No, sister. I am fine."

"It will soon be time," Nurse Bristol continued and sighed. "Don't worry, everything will be all right," she finished as she went back to sleep.

Data listened to her parents as they snored, indicating that they had slept off. She felt her mother's desperation, her pain. She knew her mother wanted grandchildren, but definitely not this way.

The day she'd found out she was pregnant had been the first day the thought of committing suicide had crossed her mind. It was so strong that if her father hadn't had the private talk with her, Data was sure that she would have killed herself. He'd urged her to love the child, that the child was a gift.

She'd listened to him as he'd cried with her. She'd wanted to tell him that it was easier said than done, but she hadn't wanted to break his heart any further. So, she'd remained silent and allowed him to cuddle her as she cried.

Every day was slightly easier to handle than the previous, but she would never forget that day, the one when she lost everything. She knew that 'til her deathbed, she was never going to forget the face of the soldier. The war had ended, and people were beginning to get on with their lives. The government was trying to rebuild and reintegrate its people back into the system. It was a new beginning, but people had no choice but to believe that it was truly the end of war and all it stood for.

For Data, it was the end of an era and the beginning of another. She knew it would break her parents' heart, but there was no way she could bring herself to physically and emotionally raise the baby inside of her. She had already told her mother, and after several arguments, her mother had accepted her decision. There was possibly no way around it.

In order for Data to survive, she had to leave the baby behind. She had it all mapped out; she was going to Lagos, and she was going to start all over again. Far away from the war, and far away from everything familiar that could remind her of what had happened. She knew it was going to be a hard journey, but it was one she was prepared to embark on.

THE AVALANCHE

"Nkechi! Nkechi! Nkechi! Please wake up."

Ikenna was finding it difficult to understand what was going on around him. Opening his eyes, he saw too many strange faces staring at him; some crying, some wailing, and some shouting, 'thank God, Welcome back.'

He couldn't understand anything that was going on, and looking around, everything seemed different. Putting his hands on his head to stop the pounding headache, he noticed a woman putting her frail hands on his shoulder flimsily.

Still confused, he asked for water and overheard them order someone whom he assumed was the maid to get him some. Standing up fully, he allowed himself to be led to a nearby chair to sit down. Looking around again, he was utterly confused as every face he saw was strange to him.

A little girl aged about ten brought a glass of water on a yellow tray. As she stretched it out to him, he thanked her as he picked up the glass. The water was rejuvenating, and sighing in relief, like a man who had journeyed a thousand miles in the desert in search of a drop, he made a mental note to tell his wife to make sure he drank lots of water everyday.

"Nkechi! Why did you scare us like that? I have told you, you have to be strong," the frail-looking old woman, who had helped him get up, spoke.

Looking at her again, he tried to remember who she was.

"Okay, ma", he replied, whilst still struggling to get to grips with the whole situation. Swallowing his inquiry, sensing that this old lady wasn't to be questioned by anybody, he remained puzzled.

Looking at the chair he was sitting on, he realised this wasn't his favorite army green reclining chair, where he sat in the evenings watching football with strict house rules that nobody else was allowed to sit on his chair, not even the president. Turning to his left, he saw a group of men, who looked like they were in their mid-forties or early fifties, and what struck him was that they were all wearing black, and they looked his way, speaking amongst themselves.

"Please, what are these men doing?" he asked the young lady who was standing by his side.

She looked at him rather strangely. "They are discussing the burial preparation of Godwin", she whispered.

"Who is Godwin?" he asked, and watched the blood drain from her face.

Whispering something he couldn't hear to the old, frail-looking lady, she turned to him. Taking his hands in hers, she ordered, "Come with me."

Still not settled after what had happened to him, Ikenna obliged. He allowed himself to be dragged as they walked into a dark room, and she switched on the light and shoved him in front of the big standing mirror.

"Look at yourself properly in the mirror, before you ask me that rubbish question again about Godwin."

The moment Ikenna looked at the mirror, he knew that he must have become mentally deranged. What he was looking at was the face and body of a woman. A woman, who had aged overnight, even though she was relatively young. She was of average height, had a round face, full bosom, but the bottom line was that he was a woman and was pregnant.

Turning around, as he looked at the lady, he muttered, "Who is this? Is this a joke?"

Glancing at the mirror again, he touched his skin.

"What are you talking about, Nkechi? This is not a joke. I don't know what has gotten into you, but you have not been behaving like yourself since you fainted. I hope you haven't caught the widow's madness," she cried. "It is going to be harder than I thought," she finished, and walking to the end of the room, she sat down on the floor, allowing the tears roll down her cheeks.

Ikenna was the most confused human being in this room. He didn't know what was happening. He was inclined to think that he had maybe been stuck with the so-called widow's madness, as the last thing he remembered before he'd blacked out was the accident. He had been on his way back from the club with his friends Emeka, Ebele, and Nonso, who were laughing at the lady Emeka had almost had sex with, by a corner of the club. Which had been prevented by the intervention of the club manager.

They had been joking about it, and he remembered feeling a bit apprehensive about Ebele's driving because they were all tipsy. He couldn't explain who was at fault or how it all happened. What he knew was that one minute the road was free and they were speeding down the Lekki-Ajah express way. The next minute, a car appeared in front of them, and it was a head-on collision. He remembered thinking that he didn't want to die before he was hit and then blacked out.

Looking at his body, or the body that he suddenly found himself in, staring at this lady sobbing on the floor, he was uncomfortable. Ikenna had never been one to sit down and let a woman cry. Whenever his wife would cry, he would always tell her to grow up and accept whatever life had dealt her. Her reply was always, *"you are a very heartless man, Ikenna. All I wanted was just a shoulder to cry on."* In the early days of their marriage, he would not respond, but after the honeymoon had ended, he'd had a response for everything, which he spewed without remorse.

Right now, he was in a different atmosphere, and he was feeling emotions he didn't even know exist. In his heart was the need for some answers.

"Please, what is my name? Where am I, and what am I doing here?" he asked the lady.

The more he spoke, the more she wailed.

"Ha! Nkechi, truly, the widow's madness has caught up with you. This is serious. We must not tell anybody. Your situation is already very bad," she finished as she danced around the room helplessly. Rubbing her hands together, she mumbled some incoherent words.

"Please, answer my questions. I need answers," Ikenna pleaded, putting both hands on top of his head as he slid to the floor, staring at the woman in the mirror.

After what seemed to be an eternity, the other lady in the room spoke. "Your name is Nkechi Gospel-John. Your husband of two years just recently passed away, after a brief illness."

Taking Ikenna's hands in hers, she went on. "I am your best friend, Doris. Today is the second day of your husband's burial rites. We have been in the village for the past week, for the funeral rites," she finished.

Ikenna wanted to laugh and say she was joking. He wanted to order her to stop playing tricks on him and please take him back to his house. He was Ikenna Obi; he lived somewhere between Lekki and Ajah in Lagos; he was a father of three boys and had a wife, Ndidi.

But the more he wanted to tell Doris or whatever she called herself who he was, the more he stared at the woman in the mirror, and it dawned on him that his soul was indeed trapped in the body of a woman. Ikenna had never felt the urge to cry, but today, right now, he wanted to wail to his heart's content.

"If my soul is trapped in a woman's body, that means Heaven has rejected me. I have no home in the spirit world," he spoke out.

Watching the apprehension in Doris' eyes, he knew that his situation was irredeemable.

Standing up swiftly from the ground, Doris looked into his eyes. "Nkechi, please, whatever happens, do not utter a word until I can speak to you again." Turning her face to the door, she called out, "Come in."

A robust woman dressed in a black beaded blouse and wrapper marched in.

"What are you doing here, Nkechi?" she demanded as she stood arms akimbo. "Your husband is dead, and you are here enjoying yourself. You have not told me what you did with my brother," she accused.

Confused, Ikenna looked up as Doris. He did need help.

"*Haba* Sister Beatrice, how can you say things like that? You should be sympathetic towards her. Her husband, your brother, just died, and she is pregnant ..."

"*Abeg* Doris, please keep your mouth shut and stay away from this matter," Beatrice screamed. Turning towards Ikenna, she continued. "I have told you, this life, you shall not enjoy it as you didn't let my brother enjoy his life," she finished, kissing her teeth as she walked out of the room. "Make sure you are outside in front of the elders within the next ten minutes," she added as she stepped out.

He turned to look at Doris.

"What did I do wrong?" Ikenna asked.

She looked hard at Nkechi. "This is why I say we shall keep your current confusion a secret. You cannot let them know that you are suffering from the widow's madness. That is your late husband's elder sister, Beatrice. When your husband was alive, we called her the old maid, because she was always a pain in the ass. She wanted to control everything that concerned you, from your husband to how to manage your kitchen; she was a monarch in your own house. The biggest fight you had with her was when you discovered a few months ago that she was a signatory to your husband's salary account."

Ikenna looked at himself again in the mirror and wondered what sort of life the woman he saw in the reflection lived. How could her sister-in-law be signatory to her husband's salary account? That was unheard of.

Looking around the sparsely furnished room again, he knew that he had to obey Doris and stick to her until he figured out a way to get out of this mess. As he walked outside quietly, he was quickly led to a corner of the room and sat down, as timid as a mouse. He wanted to retaliate. To stand up and shout at everybody who had disrespected him in the past hour of him becoming conscious, but something within him, the body of the woman his spirit occupied, would not permit him.

She urged him to be silent, to be docile, to be quiet, and not say a word. He couldn't understand how this was to be, since she wasn't even there, but he felt a great sense of foreboding that if he spoke out, if he rebelled, he was going to jeopardize the lady, Nkechi's, life. So, he kept quiet.

And so, the still small voice came back. Ndidi used to plead with him to take sides with her anytime they went on a visit to his parents' house. He would always brush it aside and tell her that she was just making a mountain out of nothing. She never wanted to be around his people. It irritated him, and so, he had threatened that if she didn't go with him to see his family, he wasn't going to see her parents.

He knew Ndidi's parents meant a lot to her, so she obeyed. She obeyed like the good wife he wanted, but in hindsight, he was just an asshole. She would go to his family house, and his mother would have loads of chores for her to accomplish with a given time frame, from washing the dirty clothes with her hands, to cooking outside with firewood, every time. He'd turned a blind eye, which was stupid of him. He couldn't understand what he'd been trying to accomplish or prove to Ndidi. She hated his sister, and he was ashamed to admit it, but this sister-in-law, Beatrice, was exactly like his sister. Using his hands to cover his face, he sighed out loud.

Ikenna looked around, observing a man who looked neither young nor old bark out orders, and people scrambled around to fulfill them. Turning to look at Doris, he beckoned to her.

"Who is that man?" he whispered.

He seemed vaguely familiar. Ikenna couldn't stop the feeling of loathing and hatred that filled his mouth like bile. Something didn't sit well with him.

"Oh, that is Brother Emma, your brother-in-law", she replied. She then searched Nkechi's face for any form of recognition, realizing that it was lost to her dear friend. "That fall you had really has made you lose your memory because if you have forgotten Brother Emma, then you really need help," Doris stated.

Stroking her friend's shoulder, she wiped the tears that ran down her face. "Don't worry, I will protect your secret, just stick with me", she finished.

Standing up to leave, she looked at her friend again, and retying her wrapper, she walked towards a group of other women.

Feeling the hair at the back of his head stand up, Ikenna turned, seeing his supposed brother-in-law, Emma, look at him, and bringing out his long tongue, Emma licked his lips gleefully. Ikenna couldn't stop Nkechi's body from shuddering uncontrollably. Something wasn't right with the way Emma looked at him. Ikenna wondered what kind of man he was. Signaling to Doris, he watched her as she excused herself from the group of women.

"What is it, Nkechi? Do you want to use the bathroom?"

Sensing an excuse to leave the oppressive sitting room, he nodded. "Yes, I do, and I need company as it is already dark. You know how I feel about the dark."

Doris watched her strangely. "Nkechi, you may be the most docile and forgiving woman I have ever met in my life, but one thing I know about you is that you are not afraid of anything, certainly not the dark. Anyway, let us go," she finished.

Standing up, she stretched out her hands, and commenting to the older women that they were going to the toilet, Doris led the way.

Ikenna, staring at his fingers intertwined in Doris' palm, still couldn't believe that he was in the body of a woman. Her hands looked as wrinkled as those of a sixty-year-old woman who had worked all her life on the farm. He sensed that she, too, had her own strength and weakness. And if Doris was right about what she said, then it was he, Ikenna, who was afraid of the dark.

It amused him that as a man in his own body, he would never have admitted it for the world, that he, the first son of Mr. Obi, father of three strong boys, was afraid of the dark. Impossible.

But today, in the disguise of a woman, he was able to finally admit this part of his life. He sensed somehow that there were other weaknesses that he was going to learn, which he wasn't looking forward to. Walking behind her, he followed as Doris led them outside the house, towards the forest. Which made him a bit apprehensive.

His boys were afaird of the dark. He would berate Ndidi for leaving the lights on whenever they were put to bed. Her answer all the time was, "*They do not like the dark. You know they sleep like rocks. When they've gone to bed, I will turn the lights off.*"

He would sigh, and then, because he had to always say the last word, he would finish up with, "*They are boys and shouldn't be scared of the dark. They aren't girls.*"

By this time, he was sure Ndidi must have had enough of him, because she would always pretend like he wasn't speaking to her and walk away.

Here he was, finally admitting that he was scared of the dark, and always had been. Growing up, he'd never had the guts to admit it, because he knew he would have been ridiculed and called a sissy all his life.

Looking again at Nkechi's hands, he hated being in this body. It was like admitting the truth and looking at life from a different angle. If he continued examining his life, he, Ikenna, didn't think he was going to like himself as a person.

"Where is the toilet, and why are we going into the bush?" he asked.

Doris turned back. "There is no toilet in Brother Emma's house."

He looked around at the dilapidated building. "Why am I not in my husband's house? *Abi*, he didn't have a house?" he asked, surprised.

Doris looked at her again, putting her fingers in her mouth. She stamped her feet in frustration as she wiped the tears from her eyes.

"Truly, my friend, Nkechi, your mind has been exchanged. I don't know how, but you are not the Nkechi I know. How can you not know the things that have happened here recently? Your husband did have a house. In fact, your house was finished last Christmas, and it was dedicated. Everybody who was around during the Christmas holidays came to witness the house opening. You had guests from everywhere attend as you served them goat meat pepper soup, pounded yam and *oha* soup. Beer and *tombo* in kegs and in abundance. Can you remember that?"

Ikenna's memory was all muddled up, but he could see people dancing in flashbacks.

"I am not so sure. I know there was a time this body of mine was happy and at peace with the world," he replied as he breathed in and out to calm his nerves as they continued walking into the dark forest.

He wanted to scream out in fright like a little child who had just watched an episode of Count Dracula, the creaking of the crickets adding to his fear.

"Well, there is even speculation that it was the lavish open house that led to the death of your husband."

"Tell me about it, every detail," Ikenna asked as he looked for a way to take his mind off the fear.

Suddenly stopping, Doris brought out a small penknife, and she cleared a bit of the stray tree branches. "You can ease yourself here. It is safer and far away from those people."

Staring at the spot, Ikenna felt like he was having the worst nightmare of his life. He wanted to ask Doris to stop the acting and come back to reality. How was he supposed to ease himself here when she was standing there staring at him?

Besides, the last time he'd used the toilet, he'd been a man. He'd been in the club, and after a couple of drinks, had known it was time to let it out. Instead of using the designated club bathroom, he'd gone outside, behind the building. Unzipping his pants, rejoicing as the fresh air had hit him, with a sigh of relief, he'd stretched, spraying his urine on the flowers beneath. He remembered laughing to himself as he talked to the flowers, telling them that they should enjoy the nutrition he was bestowing on them.

Coming back to the present, he didn't know the first thing about peeing like a woman. Sneaking his hands inside the wrapper, he touched his privates as he looked for his manhood. Feeling a sense of betrayal when he didn't find it, he sneaked a peek at Doris, grateful that she was occupied with narrating the events leading to the lavish open house and the death of Nkechi's husband.

"I remember you telling me how Godwin's dream was to build a befitting house in the village. He wanted to show everyone that he had arrived. That his hard work in Lagos had paid off. He erected the house within three months. There was even speculation that all the furnishing was imported from Italy. Is that true?" she asked.

Still struggling to bend down and ease himself, Ikenna looked up. "I am not sure, as I do not recollect."

"Well, that was the talk in the village and even amongst our friends in Lagos. It was very grand. It was one of those houses that had a big, noiseless diesel generator, the fence very high, barbed all round for extra security. The fascinating thing about it was that the gates were controlled by remote control. It was a spectacle, as everybody wanted to see how a gate could be controlled remotely. One thing I know you told me was that your favorite place in the house were the toilets. This, I found very strange. You said that for once in your marriage, your husband had listened to you and taken his time, investing richly in the bathroom and toilets. The house was a six-storey building, four rooms upstairs and two rooms downstairs, all en suite, of course. In the master bedroom, you had a Jacuzzi."

"Why were the bathrooms and toilets of great importance to me?" Ikenna asked, interrupting Doris as he finally finished easing himself, thanking Fate that he had been able to manage this scene.

"I don't know. You always had something about toilets not being done to your taste. Maybe because you usually spent the whole day in the bathroom. Can you not remember how everyone wanted to have their bath before you got into the bathroom during our university days, because once you were in there, everyone who hadn't had their bath was guaranteed to be late for their lectures?" Doris laughed.

He laughed, too. This must explain why it hurt Nkechi's body terribly that she had to ease herself in the forest and not in a proper toilet with flowing water.

"It is true, I remember that," he lied. Listening to the creaking of the crickets, he looked up to the sky, noticing that it was a full moon. A good sign or a bad sign, who could say? "Please continue," he urged.

"Well, the bottom line is that the housewarming was the talk of the town, but it was there one could see that you and your husband had a lot of enemies."

"Why? Were we terrible people?" Ikenna asked.

Since he'd woken up in this body, he had sensed that Nkechi was a likable person. He knew this because he, Ikenna, had his fair share of enemies. No fault of his, or maybe because of his big mouth, one couldn't be certain.

"I really find it hard that you do not remember this particular event because it was what changed the course of your life forever. When you got back from the village the next year, you found out you were finally pregnant after two years of fretting, and it was the beginning of Godwin's mysterious illness. It was also the moment you realized that your brother-in-law, Emma, and your sister-in-law, Beatrice, were jealous of you."

Sensing an intruder, Ikenna gripped Doris hands with fear.

"Who is there?" he asked frightfully.

"Why are you screaming like a guilty woman, Nkechi?" Beatrice sneered.

"*Haba* Sister Beatrice, what is your problem? We only just came here because Nkechi needed privacy," Doris replied, defending Nkechi, hoping that Sister Beatrice had not been eavesdropping.

Close to them now, she looked Nkechi up and down, and kissing her teeth, she continued. "You had better come back into the house, I do not trust you. You still haven't given us the papers of the house."

He suddenly felt an overwhelming urge to smack the bitterness off her face. "Which papers? And which house?"

Beatrice stood aggressively. "Stop pretending like you do not know what I am talking about. I have told you the last time I checked, Brother Emma and I were the beneficiaries of all your husband's properties, as it is supposed to be."

"Who told you that? Am I not his wife? Am I not the mother of his child?" Ikenna as Nkechi challenged, ignoring the warning look Doris was giving her.

Beatrice pointed a finger at her. "Who told you that? Which brother's wife? Can you not remember what I told you when you first got married to my brother? If you have forgotten, let me refresh your memory. In this family, you are nobody. Forget how my brother treated you. I always tried to warn you that you shouldn't believe in fairy tales, but you refused. After all, where is he now, and where are you? I have been taking it easy with you, and I must go and tell the women in the village that it is time for you to be taught a good lesson. You had better come inside and never leave my sight again," she warned as she walked away.

"Nkechi, what have you done? I told you not to say a word to this woman, and now, you have ruined your life!" Doris lamented.

"How have I ruined my life?" Ikenna replied, perplexed. "All I did was confront her. She shouldn't be saying things like that."

"*Ha!* Nkechi, forget all the things we talked about in school. Forget all this feminist talk that we always preached. Do you know what situation you are in right now?"

"No. Other than the fact that my husband is dead, I have a kicking baby growing in my stomach, and I feel like I am in the middle of nowhere, what situation am I in?" Ikenna asked, fed up with all the pretense.

He could sense that Nkechi's body pleaded with him to remain calm, but his wasn't a calm spirit; he was known as the hot head amongst his clique of friends. Only recently, he couldn't forget how he'd chased the man who'd snatched his wife's watch off her wrist in traffic. The moment he'd heard his wife scream that her watch had been snatched by a man on an *Okada,* fire had burst in his head.

Without giving it much thought, he had gotten out of the car and chased the motorcyclist 'til he'd caught up with the man. Dragging him off the *Okada,* thank goodness there was traffic, he'd beat the man senseless and would have sent him to his grave if not for the intervention of the people around. So he knew that he, Ikenna, was hot-headed.

Doris looked at her friend again, worry plastered all over her face. "Your husband is late, you do not have a child for him. Your brother-in-law, Emma, hasn't come out plainly to say it, but has been insinuating that you will have to marry him. Your sister-in-law Beatrice wants everything that was your husband's, and I am sorry to say it, God rest his soul, but your husband was stupid enough to trust his family members over you because it is very likely that you are losing everything he owned. And wait, there is news that you are responsible for the death of your husband, so my dear friend, everything is against you, and you opening your mouth isn't going to help."

"How can my in-laws have everything that my husband and I worked for? What about the law?" Ikenna asked. He couldn't understand how this was possible.

"Nkechi, you are talking like you do not live in Nigeria again, or you weren't married to a Nigerian. First of all, who is Godwin's next of kin?

Not sure what to reply, he kept his mouth shut.

"You see, you don't have an answer because frankly, you don't know. Look, let us go back, before Beatrice raises Hell." Saying this, she started walking towards the house.

Suddenly stopping, she turned towards Nkechi. "And for your information, you are in Emma's house right now because Emma, his wife, and their children have taken full possession of your house."

Staring at her sternly, hoping she understood the implication of her words, Doris continued walking towards the house. This was going to be a long journey for her friend; she feared that she wasn't tough enough to withstand the backlash when it all began.

Doris had seen the way her culture had reduced a strong woman into a spineless maggot. She had seen the way it had reduced a rich woman, with all her pride and glory, to a church rat. She hoped Nkechi really did have the backbone, because it was going to be a very tough road ahead for her.

Ikenna sighed again within. Who knows—maybe three days ago, he wouldn't have reposnded to Beatrice they way he just did. They might even have been on the same side. But right now, he was thinking about it all, and the annoyance and shame he felt for not defending Ndidi, his wife, when she'd needed him, was unbearable.

He'd seen her take shit from his family, from his sister, from his mother, and he hadn't said anything. He'd never berated them. He'd never even cared. He felt she was a woman so she should be able to take it and like it because she had to prove herself worthy of being his wife. Who did he even think he was to treat anyone like that, let alone the person he was intimate with?

Nobody deserved to be treated that way. His heart ached for his wife, Ndidi. He wanted to hold her, carry her, put her on his lap and say he was sorry for everything. She propably would give him a hard time about it, because they had drifted apart. She had grown to resent him, and he knew that. She hadn't said that to his face, but he could sense it.

Maybe it was too late for him, but he was going to try if he ever got out of this body.

"Doris how did I get to meet Godwin, and how many siblings does he have? 'Cause it seems like everything revolves around his family."

Doris stared at her, hesitating a bit, as though she didn't want to say any further. Taking Nkechi's hands, she began. "Look, you meet Godwin through a friend of ours. Godwin was Nne's brother."

"Who is Nne? Why can I not remember her?"

"I have tried to come to terms with the fact that you have suffered from amenesia, so I would try not to struggle to respond to your questions. We both had a falling out with Nne, as I attributed it to jealously. You thought otherwise, but Nne protested vehemently against you marrying her brother, and because he went through with it, she ceased all communication with both of you."

"Where is she now? Did she come for the burial?"

"No, Nkechi, she didn't. I am not even sure anyone is really in communication with her."

Ikenna stared at Doris, for what seemed like an eternity. It did look as though everybody had fought against this union.

Staring at Nkechi's body, he sighed. He hoped that Nkechi didn't even meet Godwin. Again, did her mother ever get to meet Godwin, or maybe sense the problems that would surmerge in regards to this union? All these questions saddenned Ikenna. He really hoped this wasn't it for him. He really hoped that he would be able to get out of this body and try and fix the mess he'd left behind and somehow help Nkechi find some sort of closure.

TURBULENCE

Walking back into the room, Ikenna sensed the oppression, and looking around, he was grateful that nobody came to talk to him. Closing the door behind him, he heaved a sigh of relief. He switched on the light and was grateful that there was electricity, even though he could hear the humming of the generator. He made a mental note to ask Doris who was footing the bill for the diesel.

Standing in front of the mirror again, he saw this woman called Nkechi. She wore a high-neck, plain black blouse which was almost choking her throat, the long sleeves making the garment one of the ugliest he had ever seen. Untying the wrapper, he looked at it and smelt it in disgust. It smelt of mold, human sweat, and misery, and examining it closely, he saw holes in the fabric. He wondered where they got the wrapper from, and making another point to ask Doris this, he dropped it on the bed.

As he untied the second one, the stench that oozed out from underneath almost made him gag. Catching a glimpse of the mirror again, he felt like the woman in the reflection was having a good laugh at his expense. Sitting down on the bed, he brought his mouth towards his privates, squeezing his nose as he smelt it. It was horrible. It amazed him how he was always turned on whenever he smelt a woman.

He remembered his wife would always complain that she dared not undress in front of him, because he would follow her scent everywhere. This time around, the smell was very offensive. This vagina hadn't been washed in a few days. Putting his hands inside his armpit, he smelled his fingers—the scent was pungent. It reminded him of a mouth that had chewed garlic and remained unwashed for three days.

Looking at the mirror again, he wished he could ask her a lot of questions. First of all, why, of all the bodies in the whole wide world, did his soul decide to inhabit a widow who may be going through the biggest loss of her life? Why didn't his soul find a rich man who didn't have any worries in life? Who had everything at his disposal such as women, money, and cars? He wasn't ready to fight for any woman's rights; it wasn't his passion.

Even though he was never in support of the way women were treated sometimes in society, he still was of the opinion that he couldn't make his wife his next of kin.

Feeling the lady in the mirror frowning at him, Ikenna knew that he had to get out of this body before he became a lunatic. This was his reality now, and he had to figure out a way to live with it while he searched for ways of retrieving his body. He tried to picture the expression on Doris' face if he told her that he wasn't her Nkechi, that he was a man in a woman's body. Laughing to himself, he knew there were things best kept secret.

Raising the black blouse, he touched his protruding stomach, and feeling a flutter, he shuddered. Guessing it was the baby moving, he touched his stomach again. The first time he had felt this was when he'd been in the forest with Doris. The movement was so strange. He wondered how he was going to sit still for hours while something that felt like the movement of a snake wriggled along his midsection.

As though sensing his thoughts, the baby started moving up and down his stomach again. From what he remembered, Nkechi was six months pregnant, and he didn't like it. The weight of it all was another ball game. Pulling himself upright, he watched himself walk across the room, laughing uncontrollably when he realized that he wasn't walking but waddling like a penguin.

He really must have offended the gods of his forefathers for him to be cursed with this fate, because as far as he was concerned, being stuck in a pregnant woman's body was the worst punishment ever.

Sighing to himself, he picked up the wrapper from the bed and tied it. He had to figure out a way of getting out of the situation he was in. First things first, he had to deal with being in a woman's body. Suddenly, the rumblings of his stomach made him realize that he was hungry, and so he decided it was time to seek Doris for food.

"Doris, I am very hungry. I don't think I have eaten all day," he complained.

Laughing, she replied, "Of course you have. Between me and Mama, you have been well fed." She must've seen the confused look on her friend's face. "Mama is your other sister-in-law. Her name is Ijeoma, but everyone calls her mama as she is the baby of the house," Doris explained. "Don't worry about her, she is on your side," she finished as she signaled to a young girl.

Watching a skinny girl walk towards them, in a long, straight black dress, with a black turban tied fiercely on her head, Ikenna could see a striking resemblance between her and her sister Beatrice. It occurred to him that he didn't have a clue as to what Nkechi's late husband looked like. He didn't know whether he was good-looking or not, or if he was tall or short. Judging from his older brother Emma, he could guess that Nkechi's husband may have been average in height.

"Yes, Auntie Doris," Mama called out as soon as she was close to them. Looking at Ikenna, she smiled at her.

"What is there to eat?"

"I don't really know, but I think the women have prepared yam and palm oil." She glanced at Nkechi again. "I know it isn't your favorite dish, but they said that since they are mourning, you have to eat like you are in mourning and not like you are celebrating," Mama finished, feeling sorry for her sister-in-law.

She had almost been branded a rude, spoilt Lagos girl because she'd dared to ask her sister why she was subjecting Nkechi to that sort of treatment. She had always loved her brother's wife and even looked up to her in every way. She was the most docile woman she had ever seen, married to her brother who had been very difficult, and she had had the grace to calm the storm. She didn't want to say it, but she felt that her older sister, Beatrice, was jealous of her. Sister Beatrice had always been a very bitter woman, blaming every other person for her problems and situation in life apart from herself.

"Don't worry, that's fine for me, thanks," Ikenna replied as he watched Mama disappear.

He could guess that Mama had a nice heart, and she and Nkechi got along really well. He could sense the good vibes emanating from Nkechi's body when Mama was close by. Now, he knew that Nkechi had two allies, Mama and her trustworthy friend, Doris.

Switching his weight from one buttock to the other, he waited patiently for his meal while occasionally stealing looks at the group of women sitting a few meters away. Tonight was the preparation of the wake-keeping, after which would come the burial ceremony, and he couldn't wait to get past all of this. Spotting Mama come into the room with a stainless steel plate, he sat up, his mouth salivating at the sight of the food.

Stretching out his hands, he took the plate from her. "Thank you, Mama. I really appreciate it."

"You're welcome, Sister Nkechi. Don't worry, everything will soon end, okay," she replied as she quickly walked away, avoiding her sister.

"You know it is because you are pregnant we are even serving you food with cutlery. If not, you would not have even eaten. Rubbish! When one's husband dies, it is a time for mourning, not *jollification*."

"Thank you, Sister Beatrice", Ikenna replied as he suppressed the urge to spit in her face.

He knew that if he followed his heart, he would regret his action, causing Nkechi more pain, and so, shutting his mouth was the best solution.

"We still do not know what killed my brother, but we will find out soon, so make sure you do not sleep or contact anybody 'til after this burial ceremony," Beatrice warned as she strolled towards the women in a group.

He looked at Doris. "Who are those women, and why do they keep looking at me like I am to be slaughtered tomorrow?"

"They are the *Umuada*. All of them are the female relatives in the family, from distant relations to close ones; they are the ones who will be in charge of shaving your hair."

"Me! Shave my hair, why?" Ikenna asked as he ran his fingers through the thick, lush, long kinky hair.

One of the things he'd first noticed about Nkechi was that she had very full, extra long hair. A bit busy and unkempt right now, but one of the photographs he had spotted of her in the room was of a woman with long straight hair almost touching her waist. She sensed that Nkechi didn't want her hair to be cut.

"You have to shave your hair. It is the tradition," Doris relied.

"And what if I insist that I do not want to?" Ikenna asked.

"*Ha*," Doris explained. "You really have allowed this widow madness to eat into your brains. You cannot refuse, oh. If you do, you will be classified as the one who killed her husband to inherit all that he has," she finished.

Looking at her friend again, she felt the urge to really explain to her what the consequence of her actions would be. "Look, Nkechi, as much as possible, you do not want to draw attention to yourself. Already, they are saying that you haven't cried enough. They haven't seen you wail and roll on the floor, declaring your undying love for your husband. You can't come now and start acting all feminist. I know you are a lawyer, but leave that for the white people. This is our tradition and must be upheld," Doris finished.

Discovering that Nkechi was a lawyer was a great surprise. If she was a lawyer, why then did she subject herself to all the treatments she had been facing? Why did she have to sit on the bare floor and probably sleep there, too, only with the exception that she was pregnant, she was given a bed to sleep on.

Still, that bed was one of the most uncomfortable spring beds he had ever laid on. If she was a lawyer, couldn't she have a say in whether they cut her hair or not? If she was a lawyer, why would her brother-in-law possess her husband's house, and why didn't she make sure that her husband had a will or that her husband made her his next of kin?

Doris had said this was the only way Nkechi could show her in-laws that she loved her husband and hadn't killed him. But if the roles were reversed—which they were right now—Ikenna wouldn't have minded killing Nkechi's husband with his bare hands.

"Doris, tell me, how did we become friends?" he asked.

Staring at her friend strangely, she sighed. "We have been friends since our university days. We both studied law at the University of Lagos."

"So you are a lawyer, as well?" Ikenna asked, surprised.

If she was a lawyer, why did she talk as though she couldn't do something about the law?

"Yes, I am a lawyer, but I haven't been practicing for a long time now. I do buying and selling. You remember my trips to Senegal to buy materials to sell?" Doris asked, hoping that this part of her friend's memory wasn't wiped away, as well. She was so afraid for her.

The memory loss was a good thing and a bad thing at the same time. Good thing in the sense that Nkechi could forget a lot of the problems that went on in her family between herself and her in-laws. A bad thing because, since her fainting episode, she had noticed a sense of boldness that she had never perceived before.

Her friend was the most obedient, submissive person she had ever known. The Nkechi she knew would never question the fact that she was meant to cut her hair—she would just have gone along with it, without uttering a word.

Even the way she raised her voice to her sister-in-law, Sister Beatrice, was baffling. She, Doris, was very excited and happy that for the first time, her friend had the backbone to challenge the old maid, but she couldn't dare voice her thoughts. A woman never went down that path.

"Oh, that explains a lot. Tell me about our friendship in school," Ikenna asked. He needed to know a few things about this Doris friend before he jumped into conclusions.

Since he was aware that Nkechi's body accepted Doris as a friend wholeheartedly, they must have gone though a lot of experiences together. If he was asked to describe Doris, he would say that she was a very pretty woman who did all she could to hide it.

It wasn't just the sober look she'd put on for the burial, but it was her every day look. She wore virtually no make up, had tiny earrings that were only visible when you came very close to her. She was tall and slim, her skin a russet reddish-brown. She had a very narrow waist, which curved out into small-rounded, firm buttocks.

Doris would have been a very superb model had she ventured into it, but he guessed her upbringing would never have allowed her to consider such a profession. Doris was, in fact, his friend Emeka's kind of girl. He always loved them tall and slim; he said it brought him great joy to run his hands up their long legs, in anticipation for more.

For him, he loved his women small. He wasn't particularly a very tall man, and he wanted his women shorter than himself. He hated the idea of having to stand on his toes just to steal a kiss. Thinking again of Ndidi, he knew he really had to find a way to get back to her and make everything right again. Why he let the monster within rear its ugly head in his marriage was a mystery.

One of Doris' most prominent features was her face. She had a narrow, oblong face with high cheekbones and a petite nose. She had the most piercing eyes, as though she could see through your soul when she stared at you, but sometime in her childhood, she must have been taught not to look people in the eye, because Doris was constantly staring at anything other than his eyes when she talked.

Drawing closer to her, Doris began. "When I met you, I noticed that you were very shy, and you wanted to stay on your own. I was the one who made the first move. I was looking for a roommate as I wanted to stay off campus, and I had overheard you ask the departmental secretary if she could recommend any good, safe, off-campus accommodation for you.

"We paid for an apartment together, in Akoka, just about a twenty-minute walk from the University of Lagos, and it was fantastic. You had said you wanted to lose weight, so every morning, you would walk to school and back, despite the scorching sun. I used to laugh at you, but I later got initiated into the walking ritual, and we would leave the house early every day, before sunrise, and walk to school. We would wait 'til it was no longer hot to go back to our room, using the waiting time to read and get ready for the next day of lectures."

Looking at Nkechi, Doris put her hands around her, bringing Nkechi's head to rest on her shoulder, blocking away the background music, as the village singers sang sorrowful songs.

"Tell me more," Ikenna prompted as he rested his head on Doris.

He suddenly realized that he needed this shoulder to lean on. As he heaved a sigh of relief, a heavy burden lifted off him. He felt like a little child who sat down on his grandmother's thighs as he listened to her tell stories of her childhood and growing up.

"*Ha*, you were one of the most intelligent people I had ever known, and I learnt a lot from you, and because of you, I graduated with a second class upper degree. I loved your tenacity. Not a day went by without you reading. It took me a while to know anything personal about you, though, because I think you were trying to assess whether I was a trustworthy friend even though we had been roommates for over a year.

"You told me about your mother, who was your best friend. You never knew your father, as your mother said you were born during the war. The only thing you knew about your father was that he was a soldier, and he was from the North. I loved you for that because you didn't hold it against your mother, you loved her even more. She did everything for you. Took care of you, cried with you. I saw the relationship you had with your mother, and I wanted that for myself, because even though I had a mother and father who were relatively wealthy, I never had the kind of close-knit relationship you had with your mum, and I wanted it so badly."

"Where is my mother now?"

After what seemed like a long time, Doris replied, "She is dead."

Raising his head up, he looked sternly at her.

"How did she die?" Ikenna asked, ignoring the perplexed look on her face.

He was already used to the way Doris looked at him now. He didn't blame her as it wasn't her fault. He would have behaved the same way, or even worse, if the tables had been turned. Doris couldn't understand even if he told her that the Nkechi she saw wasn't her friend.

"She was sick. She had ovarian cancer, and she didn't tell you until very late. She said she didn't want you to stop your education for her. She said she knew it was time for her to leave," Doris finished.

"How old was she?"

"She was in her seventies."

"That means she had me very late. Do you know why?"

"Yes, she did. I don't know why. I can only tell you what she told me. She said after the war, she made up her mind that she was going to have an affair with any man she met and felt a certain kind of attraction towards, because she wanted to be able to have a child who would at least keep her family lineage going, as she was the only child of her parents. Since she hadn't been lucky with marriage or love, and she was already forty.

"When the Biafran war started on the sixth of July 1967, she knew she had to act fast, before she died, and that was how she met your father. She said she really did like him, even nursed the idea that maybe if they both survived the war, they would get married and have a family together. Because of him, though, her family didn't starve, as he smuggled in eggs, fresh milk, garri, sugar, rice, and more, which she gave to her parents. This sustained her whole family and even her friends, as well.

"She said that the day she found out she was pregnant was the happiest day of her life, and the day you were born was the scariest day of her life, as they had just bombed both buildings by the side of her parents' house. She literally picked you up as soon as you were born and ran away with her mother and aunties into the forest for protection. That is why she named you Nkechinyere, meaning what God has given, and she shortened it to Nkechi, which means God's property, because she believed truly that you were God's property."

Listening to Doris, Ikenna realized that the story didnt add up. Either Doris didnt know what she was saying, or Nkechi's mother had lied to her.

Ikenna felt Nkechi's body agitate. He listened a bit, wondering why she was apprehensive. The story Doris had just narrated did not add up. Nkechi's mum had lied to her, and if he was Nkechi, he would have liked to get to the root of the matter.

Feeling a slight pinch in his belly, he shifted a bit, but the pinch wouldn't go. It continued, and then, he smiled. Nkechi didn't want him accusing her mother. He was in a woman's body—he had his mind and soul in here untouched, trapped in this body, but the body still controlled him. It was kind of like a supernatural experience, very intriguing and scary.

She knew her mother had lied to her, but she didn't want to admit it. There was more to her mother's story. Ikenna was intrigued about the war and would have urged Nkechi if he knew her to dig into it. Something happened during the war, and that thing had something to do with Nkechi and her mum. He didn't know how he thought this, but he could feel it in his bones.

Why Ikenna was this inquisitive, he couldn't explain. All he knew was that if he got out of this body, there were things he was going to try and fix, starting with his family.

"Thank you, Doris. I now know why we remained friends."

THE INTENSITY

It was the wake-keeping of Nkechi's dead husband.

Ikenna wasn't a cry baby and couldn't remember when last he'd shed a tear, as men weren't supposed to cry, but he felt that he had to let Nkechi's body take over at this point and wail for the loss of her husband. If Nkechi didn't cry, she would be categorized as a woman who didn't love her husband. With the way Beatrice, the sister-in-law, was behaving, Ikenna had a feeling that Nkechi would in fact be labeled a witch.

He didn't want to give Beatrice any indication that she had defeated her sister-in-law, Nkechi.

Getting up, he looked around, suddenly realizing that it was still the early hours of the morning, and almost everyone was asleep, mainly due to the copious consumption of palm wine by a lot of the village folks, as they claimed it helped soothe the loss of their dear brother and son.

Sneaking out of the sitting room to get some fresh air before the house became busy was the best option, and with his bladder about to burst, he virtually ran out of the building.

He couldn't comprehend why a pregnant woman had to ease herself every five seconds. It was becoming insufferable. Walking as fast as he could with the heavy weight of the baby resting on his bladder, he ran into the forest to ease himself, grateful that the day had already broken and he could see the sun begin to rise.

Making sure nobody was looking for him, he leaned against a palm tree, and as he looked up at the sky, he breathed in the fresh air.

One thing he could never take away from the village was the fresh air. The air in Lagos was quite polluted with all the cars and generators and lack of adequate greenery, whereas in the village, there were trees all around.

He loved the smell of the sand, the mud, the crowing of the cock signaling the beginning of a new day, the chattering of the villagers as they went about their everyday business whether it was to the farm or the stream to fetch water. He loved the freedom they had. The leisure with which life was taken here was in no way comparable to that of the city. Ikenna had a good life in Lagos—Lagos had been good to him since his arrival—but he couldn't deny that the hustle and bustle took a toll on him sometimes.

He still couldn't wrap his mind around the fact that his soul was trapped in a pregnant woman's body. Touching his protruding stomach, he felt the baby stir again.

The baby had been the first to wake him up, moving up and down his stomach. Even when he came to ease himself, he could still feel its movement. If this was how babies behaved, then he should never have subjected his wife to this by insisting on having many children. Ndidi had always wanted to have two kids, but he had insisted that the more, the merrier. How could she tell him, the second born of twelve siblings, to have only two children?

Placing his hands over his face, he covered it, as though he could someone cover the shame and disgust he felt with his behaviour.

He remembered that day vividly. It had been three months after the birth of his second son, Chukwuemeka, and he had been sex-starved. He was so horny that night, and he couldn't wait for his mother-in-law to retire to bed, leaving him and Ndidi in peace. He could tell Ndidi was tired, but his libido had been dictating the pace that night, with him nearly pouncing on her. As soon as she'd lain on the bed, he'd stripped off her flimsy nightgown, and when he had just been about to dive in, he'd heard her protest. She'd told him she was tired and wanted to get to bed.

She'd already been worried and had been fretting all day as she thought she had started ovulating again after seeing her period. She had told him that she was done with kids and that he should be careful, as well. He couldn't contain his anger that night.

Thinking about it, he felt very ashamed of himself because he knew that his shouting had alerted his mother-in-law who had been sleeping in the next room. He had screamed, reminding Ndidi that he was the head of the house, therefore he was the one to decide how many kids they had under his roof.

He'd told her selfishly that he wanted four kids, three boys and a girl. She'd screamed back that she wasn't going to have any more, accusing him of being very selfish and just thinking of only himself. It had been a huge fight which had resulted in them not speaking to each other for months, and although she'd finally succumbed to pressure and told him she was ready to have more children, he now understood what she meant.

She might even have been going through post partum depression, and he hadn't cared. He had only been in this body for a couple of hours, and he felt like dying from the weight of the baby. Slapping his forehead, or rather Nkechi's forehead, he swore under his breath. He really had a lot of things to sort out if he ever got out of this body.

Looking at his protruding stomach again, he wished he hadn't disturbed Ndidi. She had a right to have as many kids as she wanted; after all, it was her body, not his. Pregnancy was a potentially challenging experience, and Ikenna prayed that his soul found his body before the baby was due.

Suddenly alerted by the sound of footsteps, he quickly checked that his wrapper was tied properly as he looked up.

"Good morning, Brother Emma. Hope I didn't wake you."

Emma cleared his throat. "No, you didn't wake me, Nkechi, and please stop calling me Brother Emma. I thought I have told you to just call me Emma. No need for all this brother business."

Watching the way he chewed his chewing stick and spitting all over the place like a pregnant woman, Ikenna had to control himself from vomiting.

"Okay," he managed to reply.

If one could judge by one's brother's look, then Ikenna would have to conclude that Nkechi's husband had not been attractive, as Brother Emma looked like a replica of a small stout bottle.

Clearing his throat again, Brother Emma walked in circles, before settling directly in front of Ikenna.

"Ehen Nkechi, I wanted to ask you if you have thought about my proposal?" he asked, grinning sheepishly.

"What proposal? I do not know what you are talking about," Ikenna replied as he tried to get free from Brother Emma.

He wanted to smack the man right on his face, but he had to be gentle. It was getting harder to remember that Nkechi wasn't a vicious person.

"How can you say you cannot remember?" Brother Emma asked. Angry that he was being dismissed in a manner befitting a goat, he went on. "You must stop playing games and give me your response after my brother's body has been laid to rest. Because it is either you accept to be my wife, or you are left with nothing, as I am the beneficiary of all of Godwin's property." He sneered. Spitting once again, he walked away. "Better make a wise decision. If not, you and that brat in your stomach will be homeless, and you will only have yourself to blame," he finished as he walked away.

Ikenna was left speechless. He sensed that Nkechi was apprehensive. Did she really believe her brother-in-law, that she would become homeless? What was it about this family? How could all Godwin's property be given to his older brother? What had Godwin been thinking? Didn't he know that he had a wife and an unborn child to take care of?

He had to ask Doris. She seemed to be the only one who could help fill in the missing pieces of the puzzle, and suddenly, the serenity of the village was like an irritating toothache that would never cease.

"Where have you been? I have been looking all over for you. You know you have to be careful about where you go to," Doris cried as she pulled him to the backyard of the house.

"Good morning to you, too, Doris. Is there a problem?"

"You know I cannot protect you all the time. Please promise me you won't go anywhere without letting me know."

"Doris, you know I cannot promise you—"

"Promise me, I insist," Doris interrupted with a loud voice. Looking around, she made sure they were alone. "Your life is in great danger. I can sense it, and I would never forgive myself if I did not try my best."

Taking her hands in his, he squeezed them.

"Okay, I promise," Ikenna reassured her.

"Thank you. Now let us go back inside and observe the remaining burial rites."

Holding back, Ikenna drew her attention. "Doris, please explain this to me. I had a visit from Brother Emma. He was saying things like I am supposed to marry him. Tell me he was still drunk from all the drinking last night and was talking gibberish?"

Observing her friend, Doris didn't know what to do; she was in a lot of trouble. Doris couldn't see how she was going to survive when the burial rites were over and everybody had gone back. There was only little she could do for her.

"Nkechi, he isn't talking gibberish. He means everything he says, and he has your husband's entire family supporting him. The only person that isn't in support is Mama, but she doesn't have a say in all this as she is the last born and a woman just like us."

He shook his head vigorously, tired of hearing this thing about them only being women.

"Doris, tell me this is a lie. How can I marry his brother? I do not even like Brother Emma. Doesn't he have a wife? Why does he get possession of all my husband's property?" Ikenna asked, confused.

Doris looked around again. "Wait here for me, I am coming," she ordered.

He tried to figure out where she was going to, only to see Doris disappear into the kitchen and reappear within minutes with a small, wooden kitchen stool, dusting it with her hands as she placed it on the floor and patted the stool.

"Sit down. We have some minutes to talk before the whole house starts buzzing with activities," she finished as she sat down on top of a stone which had been converted to a makeshift kitchen stool.

Without a word, Ikenna sat down, sensing that the news he was going to hear was going to change the course of his life, or rather, Nkechi's life, forever.

"Nkechi, even though you are a lawyer, you are first an Igbo wife, who adhered to traditions. Things like making sure you were the next of kin wasn't top of your priority list. I remember the last time we talked about this next of kin issue; you had just discovered that years before you had married him, Godwin and his sister had a joint account. It was unbelievable, but his sister was signatory to his salary account. You had protested, telling him that it wasn't right, but he brushed it off and said it gave him an opportunity to take care of his sister who was always looking out for him. You both had a huge fight about all this, and I was called in.

"I begged you to understand him and leave him be so that in his own time, he, Godwin, would change everything. I told you that you should focus on your marriage as you had just suffered from yet another miscarriage. I shouldn't have told you that. Maybe I should have encouraged you more to be a little bit aggressive. If I had known that not only did Beatrice have access to your husband's bank accounts, your brother-in-law is also his next of kin."

The desperation Nkechi's body felt could be reflected on her face, because Ikenna watched the way Doris fretted. How could this woman have left things to chance? Was she not a lawyer? Why did she allow her sense of tradition to override common sense? Who sat down and watched while her husband's people took everything she had?

He'd always thought his wife prone to storytelling whenever she came home with one of her talks about a friend who had recently become a widow and had been thrown out of her husband's house by her in-laws. She would always rant and rave and wail and beg him to please not leave her penniless if he decided to die before his time. It had always annoyed him, with him telling her all the time that he was going to live up to a ripe old age and he wasn't going to die young.

He knew that she had a right to be afraid, because as a businessman, he had done well for himself, and he was the envy of his peers, but he could never bring himself to change his next of kin. At least, he'd tried a little when he'd put all the properties he had in his sons' names.

The more Ikenna thought about it, the more he couldn't deny the fact that he had been a selfish man.

"So what am I going to do?" he asked. There had to be a way out for this woman. "Why can I not take him to court, in fact, take all of them to court?"

Suddenly interested in the ground, Doris remained silent.

"Doris, am I not talking to you?" Ikenna prompted.

After a long time, she answered. "You weren't legally married to Godwin."

"What do you mean?" Ikenna screamed. This was sheer madness, not being legally married.

"You only had the traditional marriage, and you never had a court marriage. That is why I said before that traditions overrode your knowledge of the law."

"Then I must have been the most stupid lawyer to ever live on planet Earth. How could I not have been married legally? How is it that my brother-in-law was next of kin and now stands the chance of inheriting everything if I do not agree to marry him?"

"My sister, please don't worry your head about this now. Just be strong. Today is the wake, and you have done so well thus far. They will lay his body to rest tomorrow, and then, everything will be over. Right now, just please endure everything in silence, and after this, we will find a way. We always do," Doris finished as she squeezed Nkechi's shoulder in reassurance. Standing up, she stretched out her hands. "It is time to go inside."

Contemplating whether he should take it or not, Ikenna stood up, placing his hands in Doris'.

"There just has to be another way," he finished as he allowed himself to be led to the house.

THE UNKNOWN

The house was bubbling again with all the villagers trooping in and out as they were treated to hot bowls of pounded yam and white soup. Sensing his stomach rumble again, Ikenna knew it was time to eat.

Quickly asking Doris for some food, he sat down in a spot in the corner of the sitting room as he observed everything whilst waiting for his meal. He was made to understand that because he was—or rather, Nkechi was—carrying their grandchild, she was being fed properly.

Taking the plate from Doris, he thanked her as he dove into the bowl with all seriousness. He had to satisfy this unquenchable hunger. Now he understood why his wife was always eating like a glutton whenever she was pregnant. It had always irritated him the way she followed food like a fly that followed the smell of human waste. Sometimes, he would complain and purposely ignore her pleas to stop by the roadside to buy Udara, from the Hausaman who always had a wheelbarrow filled to the brim with the bittersweet African cherry.

Now he knew why she wanted to eat all the time. Being pregnant wasn't a day's job. If he ever got out of this body, he wasn't going to disrespect any pregnant woman again. Looking around once more, it suddenly dawned on him that this Nkechi lady didn't seem to have any relatives. Beckoning on Doris, he waited patiently 'til she came.

"Where is my family?" he whispered, as according to tradition, her voice wasn't supposed to be heard, except only when she was wailing for her loved one.

Looking at her intently, Ikenna thought that by now, Doris would have gotten used to all the questions he was asking.

"You do not have any. Didn't you hear me? Your mother was an only child, and you are her only child, and she died shortly after you married Godwin, so you have no siblings or uncles or aunties. That is why we became very good friends. You always said I was the sister you never had," Doris finished.

Ikenna could sense that Doris had a special place in Nkechi's heart, but he didn't know anything about her. All he knew was that she was a very pretty, tall lady who hid behind a terrible fashion sense.

"What about you, Doris? Where is your family?"

Heaving a frustrated sigh, Doris sat down on the floor. "I do have family, but they aren't here. They live in Lagos."

"And ..." Ikenna prompted. He had this impression that this was a touchy subject for her.

"I am married, but since I do not have any children, I am now competing for my husband's attention with his second wife and her kids."

Did life have to be a bitch? This was the first time he had really seen Doris this sad. "Look, Doris, you do not need to tell me anything you don't want to. I understand."

"I do, Nkechi. You already know everything, even more than my own sister."

"Why didn't you just walk away from the marriage?" he asked.

Doris laughed. "Nkechi, stop talking like that, abeg. You know that as a good African woman, I am not supposed to walk out of my marriage."

"But a man is allowed to?"

"See, Nkechi, let us stop talking about me and stick to what's important, making sure you are in one piece during and after your late husband's burial," Doris finished, irritated, as she walked away.

Ikenna kept quiet for the first time as he listened to Nkechi's body. Nkechi felt distressed, as though she was alone and deserted. It was hard for him to understand what it meant to be an only child, because he always had his siblings around. He remembered how they would fight and quarrel for the bicycles or whatever toys his father slaved to buy or construct.

He remembered the day he'd fought with his older brother, Nna, over a bicycle. His father had just come back from the farm with an old bicycle, telling them that he had bought it for them from Mazi John and that they were to share it equally amongst themselves. That was one piece of advice he felt his father should never have given. How could six boys, aged four to eighteen, share a bicycle equally?

As usual, his older brother commandeered the bicycle, claiming that since he was the first son, he was the one who could ride it. This pissed him off. Always the hot head, he challenged his brother, and they got into a physical fight, to the distress of his mother.

He fought his brother with everything he had, but his brother, who was stronger than he was, beat him black and blue. If not for the intervention of their mother, who found herself in between them and ordered Nna to kill her since he wanted to kill her son, he was sure his brother was going to beat him into a coma that fateful day.

He recollected another incident during the Christmas festival when their numerous uncles had come back from Europe with all their nice goodies. He had looked forward to this day because it was one of the few days as kids when they ate and played to their satisfaction. They would have jollof rice and chicken.

Every Christmas eve, his mother would give him or his brother some money to go and buy a live chicken from Mazi Obi who kept a poultry. That year, it was very special because his mother had given him enough money to buy about four chickens, which implied that they each were going to have a huge piece of chicken.

He had hurriedly gone to the market to buy the chicken, pleading with his older brother Nna to help him kill the chickens as he couldn't do it, a secret his brother knew and blackmailed him with. Knowing that if anyone in the village knew that he, Ikenna, was afraid of killing a chicken, he was going to be severely mocked by his peers.

They all waited anxiously for the meal to be ready, salivating as he was handed a full plate of rice with a huge piece of chicken placed right on top. Ikenna had found a comfortable place under the palm tree to demolish his food and was at it when his brother appeared in front of him, claiming that he, Ikenna, had promised him his piece of chicken because he had killed the chickens.

Ikenna knew this was impossible and a fat lie, because he could never do that. Nobody missed this treat, not even his father. After accusing his brother of lying, Nna had spat into his food.

Ikenna had seen stars that day as his head had exploded in anger. He'd quickly pounced on his brother, enduring all the blows the other boy dished out, in order to protect his prized possession. He'd come out with a swollen eye, but he'd made sure that he didn't give his brother his chicken piece.

So, he knew what it meant to have siblings. He knew what it meant to fight for everything one wanted. He could relate to that. What he couldn't relate to was being an only child. Right now, he knew that Nkechi was lonely. She needed a shoulder to help carry the weight.

***

Ikenna sat down at a corner of the room while Godwin's—Nkechi's late husband's—body was laid for the wake. He had been embalmed thoroughly by the morticians and didn't look anything like the portrait of him. Looking at the portrait, Ikenna tried to understand what had drawn Nkechi to him. He could feel her body urging him to wail and cry.

Ikenna was never an emotional person as he could never cry. Even the day he'd stepped on a nail in the village when he was younger, he hadn't cried. That day, he'd been running away from Nna who had been chasing him with a cutlass, screaming 'I will show you who is older,' his mother running after them screaming at Nna to have mercy and not kill her son for her. He, Ikenna, had been laughing while running, basking in his running skills, for he could outrun his older brother any day.

He hadn't seen the nail. It was as though the gods had left it there on purpose to teach him a lesson of some sort about respect.

He could never forget the excruciating pain he'd felt the moment he'd stepped on the rusty nail.

Hopping on one foot, he was screaming, *'Anwuolam ooo, I am dead ooo.'* This had alerted his family. His mother, ever the drama queen, had started screaming at Nna that he had finally killed her son. She'd already started saying her rosary, because his mother was an avid Catholic, begging Mary, the mother of Jesus Christ, to spare her son from any leg amputation.

Hearing all the commotion, his father had come out, and on assessing the situation, he'd quickly ordered that Ikenna be brought to his side, giving him strict instructions not to cry, telling him that a man never cries. Ikenna, with the aid of a stick in his mouth, had endured the wrenching pain as his father had brought out the rusty nail from his foot and then poured Gordon's dry gin on it to stop the infection. The pain had been indescribable.

"Take heart, my sister. It is the will of the gods," a lady told Ikenna as she tapped his shoulders in sympathy.

Touching his face, he realized that he was crying. Nodding to the lady, he wiped the tears off his face. Yet, they continued to roll down.

Sometimes, he couldn't understand this body he was in. He could control it sometimes, but most times, it acted like it had a mind of its own, which was a bit uncomfortable for him. He had willed himself to stop crying, but he could feel that this body didn't want it. Nkechi wanted to be given the right to cry her heart out for her late husband, and she wasn't letting anybody stand in her way. So Ikenna just sat down as the tears rolled all down. Even when he heard the screams coming from his mouth, he was inwardly amused.

He wanted to laugh and ask his maker if this was a joke; he wanted to be transported back to his body immediately.

"You haven't cried like this in a long while, Nkechi. Don't hold back any more, release it, it is good for you," Doris advised as she sat down beside her. Taking her in her arms, she rocked her from side to side as the tears continued rolling down.

"Thank you," Ikenna replied for lack of anything to say.

He wanted to scream at her that she should stop what she was doing as he wasn't mourning anybody. He wanted to stand up and run away, far away from this place and think of his life.

"What was Godwin like?" he asked Doris, instead.

"Where do I start from?" she retorted.

"Start anywhere," he whispered.

"Okay. You had just broken up with Ugo, your university boyfriend; this was just before we went for our National Youth Service. I had told you that you could try dating men from other tribes, since your past two boyfriends had been Igbo, and you said no, that you couldn't see yourself marrying any man who wasn't Igbo. You said that you could marry from another village, but the guy must certainly be from Igboland.

"I laughed at your strong words, and amused, I tried to dissuade you from that position, but you stood by it, and so, you didn't show any of the Yoruba guys that came around any green light. This happened until one day, a friend of mine invited us for a party. Her family was celebrating her brother who was coming back from the United Kingdom. Coincidentally, it was also his thirty-fourth birthday."

"Don't tell me the friend's brother was Godwin?"

"Yes, my friend's brother was Godwin. And that was where the love match started. You were in awe of him. I couldn't believe it because, first of all, he wasn't your spec."

"What was my spec?" Ikenna asked, curious.

"You always liked your men tall and huge. Godwin was the opposite. He was of average height, truthfully, borderline short. He wasn't robust, actually quite skinny, but I don't know what you saw in him. Maybe his smile, because you kept remarking on his smile and saying that he had the most gorgeous smile you had ever seen.

"Well, before I could say *Jack Robinson*, you told me that you were getting married to him. In fact, you were already pregnant, so nobody could talk you out of the union. Your mother was happy that finally, she was going to carry her grandchild before she died. His people were very happy."

"Including Sister Beatrice?" Ikenna asked.

If everybody was happy about Nkechi and Godwin's union, then why was it that he could sense malicious vibes from Godwin's older brother and sister?

"Yes, they were, including Sister Beatrice. She pretended to love you. You didn't see her true colours until after the wedding. It was because you were pregnant that you didn't legalize your marriage. You said you didn't want to be a pregnant bride and that you would legalize it after the baby's birth, but it never came."

"What happened to the baby?"

Looking at her friend again, Doris placed her hands on Nkechi's forehead.

"Why did you do that?"

"Nothing, my friend. You had a miscarriage when you were four months pregnant, which was a strong blow to you and Godwin. It was from this moment onwards that Sister Beatrice reared her ugly head. She asked you to follow her to one prophet, who was going to pray for you, after which the baby you lost would come back to life and you would give birth in nine months, but you refused. Then, she began accusing you of wanting to deny her brother the right to being a father."

"And where was Godwin in all this?" Ikenna asked, curious.

Even though he had come to terms with his selfishness towards his own wife, he didn't take any rubbish from his family. He kept them in their place most times, but when it suited him, the small voice reminded him. An incident which he took control over had been when his older brother Nna's wife had paid a visit to them.

While Ndidi had been preparing their meal, Nna's wife had scolded her for chopping the okro with a knife instead of blending it. This had caused a huge quarrel, which had led to him kicking his brother's wife out of his house, and he'd been very happy doing that, as he had never liked his brother's wife, anyway. But he still allowed his sister and mother to treat Ndidi any how they wanted. Yes, he could see similar traits in Godwin's family, in his own family, and his foolishness.

He remembered the first year of his marriage to Ndidi. He had gone to the village to celebrate Christmas, ignoring her plea that they shouldn't spend their Christmas holiday in the village. He'd refused, and they had traveled to the village. There was no way he was going to listen to her at that time—he had to show his village friends that Lagos had indeed been generous to him. Even if he had left the village to be an understudy for his uncle who owned a provisions store in Balogun market, he was now a certified accountant working for one of the most influential financial houses in Lagos.

He'd wanted to show his village friends that he, too, had learnt to talk like a man who lived in Lagos and could drive all the four wheels in the world. He'd wanted to show his friends and his older brother that money wasn't a problem for him, so he had insisted that they go to the village.

If he ever got back to his body, if he ever saw Ndidi again, he was going to apologise profusely to her.

That Christmas had been the worst holiday ever! His mother had insisted that Ndidi wake up before dawn and go to the stream in the village to fetch water. She had insisted that she balance the big bucket of water on her head, the proper way, but Ndidi had fumbled a lot. She hadn't been brought up that way; she was a city girl who hardly visited the village.

He knew he could have told his mother to stop it, but he had not, and had allowed Ndidi to suffer for years, 'til the death of his mother. How could he call himself a man when he had allowed this to go on for years? Why did he even turn a blind eye to all the mistreatment? He really had to find a way to atone for his sins.

"Nkechi, I don't want to speak ill of the dead, but your Godwin turned a blind eye. Anyway, I better leave now. Sister Beatrice has been stealing glances at us. You know you are not supposed to talk. Let me go and get you some food." Saying this, she stood up and left.

Looking at Sister Beatrice, Ikenna could see the viciousness in her eyes. Sister Beatrice was an epitome of wickedness. He wasn't afraid of Sister Beatrice. He knew he could handle her very well, but it was Nkechi he feared for. She was scared and afraid, he could sense it.

He wanted to reassure her. He wanted her to know that he had her back and that she should not worry; everything was going to be all right. He wanted to ease her pain, because this good woman had suffered at the hands of the people she trusted and called family.

Trying to ease the back pain he had been enduring for some time, he signaled to Mama to please bring him a pillow, and he allowed her to put the pillow behind his back. Thanking her, he held her hands, and patting the vacant seat beside him, he mentioned to her to sit down.

"Sister Nkechi, how are you?" Mama whispered.

"I am fine," he replied.

Looking around at first, as though trying to gauge if she should talk or not, Mama turned back to look at Nkechi. "Sister Nkechi, you know that once they lay my brother to rest, your trouble starts."

"How do you mean?" Ikenna guessed what she was saying, but he wanted to be sure.

"Sister Beatrice and Brother Emma have already decided what they want to do with you. All Brother Godwin's properties will be shared between them," Mama sobbed. "I don't know how they can think like that. I tried to stop them, or should I say, reason with them, but it seemed like I was just talking to deaf people. They even warned me and accused me of disrespecting them. What are you going to do, sister?"

"I don't know—"

"And didn't I tell you to get me some food to eat?" Beatrice bellowed at Mama, interrupting Ikenna.

She stood up quickly.

"Sorry, sister. I am on my way now," Mama finished quickly as she hopped away.

Watching Sister Beatrice sit down on the chair next to him, Ikenna had to suppress the urge to push her to the ground.

"What do you want, Beatrice?

"*Hmmm*, Nkechi, you have the mouth to talk to me. Anyhow, I am no longer Sister Beatrice but Beatrice, from your mouth. You can be laughing now. Is it because Godwin's friends are here you feel you can talk anyhow? Tomorrow is the final day, isn't it? After he is laid to rest, then you will see what will happen to you. Useless woman," she hissed as she stood up, walking away.

If this were a different scenario, Ikenna would have laughed at Beatrice's actions. She just behaved like a spoilt rotten little girl, not like the forty-five-year-old woman she was. Looking at Godwin's picture again, Ikenna wondered why Nkechi had allowed this man get away with what he'd done to her for so long. Why didn't he ever defend her?

Why did he allow his family to oppress her? Ikenna wanted to encourage Nkechi, but he didn't know how. He could sense her anxiety; he could sense the fear within, the desperation. She had nobody and didn't want to face her new world alone.

He wanted to talk to her, tell her that everything was going to be all right, but he didn't know how. So long as he was stuck in this body, it seemed like there was nothing he could do.

THE UNFORESEEN

The day had finally come to lay Godwin to rest, and Ikenna experienced the urge to wail and cry and beg him to come back. No longer fighting Nkechi's body, he allowed the tears to stream down her face as her mouth opened on its own accord calling on Godwin, asking him why he had deserted her this way.

In truth, Godwin had really deserted her. She had slaved for him, and all he'd done was leave her with nothing. Leave her to the wolves, his family who couldn't wait for their brother's body to be buried before they pounced on all that he'd had.

As she followed the women and they walked to the graveside, Ikenna felt a sense of desperation for Nkechi. He knew because his spirit was virtually upholding this body. He was praying that she, too, wouldn't fall down and die, as he still hadn't discovered how he was going to get back to his body and his life.

"Good morning, Sister Nkechi," Pamela called out as she walked by her side.

Looking at her, Ikenna wondered why she'd come. All this while, Nkechi's brother-in-law's wife, Pamela, had avoided her like a plague.

"Good morning, Pamela," he replied, grateful for all the information Doris had dished out.

"So, where will you live when all this is over?" Pamela asked.

Ikenna didn't really blame Pamela as she was a jealous, frustrated, unloved wife, with the ugliest dentition he had ever seen, so she had every reason to hate the woman her husband was lusting after.

"Why are you interested?" he asked sarcastically.

She kissed her teeth. "Didn't I tell you that your high handedness was going to stop one day? After the burial rites, you will not be talking to me with your nose up any more," she spat and walked away.

Ikenna didn't feel that Nkechi deserved all this hatred. The only crime Nkechi had committed—if there was a crime—was marrying Godwin. From what Doris had told him, Nkechi had tried several times to be friends with Pamela, but it had always been unsuccessful. It was as though anytime Nkechi tried, Pamela's hatred increased.

The situation that struck a chord in Ikenna was the incident about the dress. Apparently, Nkechi who had always been kindhearted had bought a few expensive dresses for Pamela when she'd traveled to Spain on holidays. Pamela had taken offense, calling a family meeting and insisting that Nkechi apologise to her for insinuating that she was ugly and poor. Nkechi, who had been stubborn about it, had refused to apologize as she hadn't done anything wrong.

She had later apologized to please Godwin, but it had completely ruined whatever had been left of her desire for a relationship with Pamela.

"What is wrong with her?" he asked Doris. He wanted to be sure there weren't more cockroaches in the cupboard.

"Hmmm, well, it's a long story."

"Another long story. Since I can see that you will tell me, anyway, so shoot," Ikenna prompted. He had to give it to Doris, she had been a strong help.

"Your brother-in-law, Brother Emma, was the one who paid for Godwin to be an understudy in Lagos."

"But I thought you said that Godwin saw himself through school."

"Yes, I did, and he could only have done that because he was an understudy, and he was very diligent. Whatever way you look at it, though, Brother Emma sees it as Godwin's responsibility to look after himself and his family. Why do you think you and Godwin were always sending money to the village?"

By this time, they had gotten to the graveside, so Ikenna allowed the *Umuada* to come and take him to the front of the grave as the priest began. He observed that a lot of people were crying and chanting that Godwin had gone and left them. It was a bit comical to watch, as half of these people wailing probably did not know Godwin. The other half were the ones Ikenna sensed had caused a big ruckus about Nkechi performing the dust to dust scene on the corpse, because they had said it wasn't a woman's right.

They were all pretenders; all were here for what they could get. As he looked around, his eyes locked with Brother Emma's, and he watched as he smiled viciously. Couldn't anyone else see that Brother Emma was evil and greedy? How did Brother Emma think that his younger brother's wife was going to be willing to marry him, sleep with him, and bear children for him? Nobody here had even asked about the baby. They were all concerned about what they would get.

Ikenna remembered back in his village when one of his aunties had lost her husband and how desolate she'd looked. She, too, had been living in Enugu. She had thought everything was going to be sorted out without problems, and coincidentally, she had also been a lawyer. When her husband was alive, she had always been nicknamed barrister, but when he died, everything changed for her. He remembered his mother taking food to her and consoling her. Telling her to be strong, and that it was the fate of every woman when she cried asking why everything had been taken from her.

He remembered his mother narrating the story to his father, saying that it was because of her stubbornness her in-laws had kidnapped her children, blackmailing her into coming to the village, where she was beaten by her sister-in-law, forced to wear sackcloth, and taken to the native doctor to swear that she wasn't the one who'd killed her husband.

At the time, Ikenna remembered that he had wondered why they were giving a woman who had just lost her husband all the stress. He remembered his auntie being stripped naked as she'd tried to defend herself from her vicious sisters-in-law, who had taken turns in pushing her around.

The final straw that broke the camel's back had been when they'd shaved her hair after her husband had been lain to rest. His auntie had wailed uncontrollably, but she hadn't protested. She'd stayed in the village for about a month with her in-laws and her three small children, enduring all types of torture and humiliation from them without protesting. He, Ikenna, as young as he'd been then, had felt very bad that these wicked people had succeeded in breaking his aunt's will, but he knew if anything happened to him, Ndidi would face almost similar circumstances.

They had reduced his auntie to a puppet who did as she was asked, cowering behind her children anytime she was spoken to. Little did any of them know that his auntie had been plotting her getaway plan, until it happened. She had gone to the stream with her children, in the guise of going to fetch water and giving them a bath. Since her in-laws were lazy and did not care if the children ate, let alone had their bath, she was finally allowed to leave the house without an escort. His aunt never came back to the house.

They searched the whole village for her, but they couldn't find her. Ikenna remembered feeling amused that her in-laws actually looked worried that she couldn't be found. They bemoaned their brother's children being kidnapped, making the whole village send out a search party. When evening came, everybody including his mother had trooped to the village police station to report a *missing person's claim*. The police said they would do all they could, but their best wasn't good enough, and she wasn't found.

Months turned into years, and nobody knew anything about her, until one day, the gods smiled on the native doctor, Uzoma, who told the villagers that his auntie had run away to be with her brother somewhere in America and that they would never set eyes on her again, nor her children. When they cried asking him to find ways to bring her back so that their brother's children would not be lost to them forever, the native doctor told them to bring five chickens, five goats, five kola nuts, and five bottles of Gordon gin for him to perform a particular ritual which was the best in summoning home lost children.

Ikenna knew that 'til date, despite all the sacrifices done, nobody had set their eyes on either his auntie or her children. He wished that Nkechi had the guts to run away from these people and cut all ties to them. He would have suggested she move out of her house in Lagos to somewhere unknown, but Lagos wasn't as big as one thought. It was easier to find her in Lagos, and Ikenna liked to think that it was easier for a native doctor to spot her in Lagos and bring her back home than if she was far away in the white man's land.

He looked around, wondering who would help Nkechi when it was time to execute her plan. Doris, yes, but she would try her best to discourage Nkechi, as well, because she, too, was a traditionalist to the core and upheld tradition. Mama, Nkechi's sister-in-law, would help, but Ikenna didn't want to get her into trouble. After all, they were her family; they were all she had since both her parents had passed away.

After the priest had finished, Ikenna allowed himself to cry. He knew that was what Nkechi wanted the most, to have the opportunity to mourn her husband, and he indulged her.

He allowed himself to cry, screaming that he wanted to be buried with the body. With the way the *Umuada* held onto him, Ikenna knew he had finally convinced the villagers that Nkechi indeed was in love with her husband and missed him.

There and then, he made up his mind that if he was ever going to get back into his body, he was going to make sure that the women close to him were treated like equals. He was going to right the wrongs he had done to Ndidi. He had to put things in place between him and Ndidi, especially legally.

He remembered those days she would have slaved in the kitchen and when she presented the food, he would decline it, saying that it wasn't good enough, thereby forcing her to go back into the kitchen and spend more hours cooking. She hated him for that, he could tell, but it hadn't bothered him then. Only now did it.

He'd never considered himself a bad man. He was a man who knew his duty and his place and stuck by it. He made sure his family was well taken care of because despite being brought up in a poor home, his hard work had paid off, as he had a departmental store which he ran alongside his wife, and a corporate job in a financial house. He hadn't been one to waste money on yearly vacations like most of his friends and his wife's friends. In fact, whenever his friends insulted him and labeled him stingy, he laughed along with them.

If one worked very hard, one should play very hard. He should have at least had more time for the kids, invested a little more in their welfare instead of just making sure they had their school fees paid for and food on the table. He should have learnt to like what they liked, asked them a few things about their school and what was happening in their lives in general instead of barking orders at them all the time.

In general, he should have just tried to be a nice guy and not callous. Nobody really wanted what was his. All Ndidi wanted was some more understanding and love. What his kids wanted was a dad who didn't bark orders or just the school fees guy, but the dad who was there for football practise, school debates, their first bicycle rides. A dad who took them to the mechanic, a dad who had discussions with his boys and truly listened to them. Above all, a dad who would show them what it was to love a woman.

Godwin had finally been laid to rest. Ikenna sat still, allowing the *Umuada* to scrape Nkechi's head. Looking at the mirror, one thing was certain—Nkechi wasn't one of those ladies who cut their hair and still looked as sexy as a wild vixen. She was a lady who always had to have hair on her head, no matter how short, to be pretty.

"So, Nkechi, have you thought about my proposal and come to a decision yet? It is already getting late," Brother Emma resumed.

"*Haba!* Brother Emma, how can you be asking about that, when your brother is still fresh in his grave. You haven't given him the opportunity to begin his journey to the great beyond," Ikenna choked as he tried not to bite off Brother Emma's humongous lips.

Even though this was none of his business, he was pleased that Nkechi had married the better-looking brother. Where Godwin was of average height, with broad shoulders, high cheekbones, white set of teeth, and a dimple to seduce any female when he smiled, Brother Emma was very short, had a robust beer belly, bald head, round flat face, broad, humongous, and very rumpled lips.

If Nkechi was Ikenna's sister and she brought this man to her house as her husband to-be, he would have opposed the wedding from Day One.

"Nkechi, I do not know what you are doing,' he replied as he straightened up, standing erect. "You act like someone who has all the options in the world, which you do not have. I have said, if you do not choose me as your husband, you and this bastard child will live in penury for the rest of your life. Even though I have secretly admired you and wished you were my wife, I cannot take such insults from you."

He marched out of the house towards the council of elders, joining them swiftly as they drank and chatted.

Taking his leave, Ikenna walked into the room. The protruding stomach was weighing on him like a sack of rice, and his feet had swollen up, like a person who was suffering from elephantiasis. Putting his hands on his pelvis, he tried to reduce the pain as he laid on his back, hoping to catch an hour's sleep.

Thirty minutes later, he couldn't control the pain any longer. The sharp agony seizing his body seconds apart was extreme, and he couldn't take it any more. He screamed for Doris to come and help. As usual, she rushed in. Seeing the look on her face, he knew that Nkechi was in a bad situation. Yet, sadly, he felt as though he was the one that had failed her.

"What is it, Doris?" he hissed as he tried to control the pain.

She looked up at Nkechi with fright painted on her features.

"You are bleeding all over the bed. I hope you are not losing the baby. Let me send someone to call the midwife in the other village," she spoke as she ran out of the room.

Trying to find a more suitable position to rest, Ikenna turned to his side as he endured the pain. It became more and more unbearable. He felt as though his stomach was going to tear apart.

Opening his legs, he tried to look in between them, which was almost impossible because of his stomach. Was this labor? Could he be experiencing what women have been going through for centuries? He couldn't believe this was how painful it was, for during the birth of his kids, he hadn't been present. It was not compulsory for the man to be in the theatre when his wife gave birth, and so, he'd never bothered to be there.

He'd always allowed Ndidi and her mother to handle it. All he did was fill his house with all sort of drinks, ordering goat meat pepper soup as he invited all his friends to come and drink and be happy with him as his wife was giving birth yet again to another boy.

If he had to go through this pain for every delivery, he would never in his life have children.

This time, he didn't need to be prompted by Nkechi's body to cry; he cried of his own accord. He wailed like a baby and prayed that this cup would pass him by, for this was worse than torture.

THE UNATTAINABLE

Waking up was a relief and a disappointment for Ikenna. Looking around, he saw his wife's face, the worried look on her features, as she screamed his name. Closing his eyes, he knew he was finally back. Opening his eyes again, he heard a male voice.

"Praise God! He is awake. Doctor, thank you!"

He heard Ndidi scream as she started crying and praying at the same time. Laughing within, it dawned on him that he was back in his body, at last. Touching his stomach, he couldn't feel the pregnancy bump, and in a way, he missed it as it had become a part of him. Some sort of spiritual connection he had with Nkechi.

Wondering what would happen to Nkechi, he felt a sense of loss. It wasn't like he wanted to be stuck in her body for the rest of his life, but he missed her. She had become some sort of sister to him. He had gotten to know a lot about her by being in her body. He'd gotten to know a lot about how women analyzed, viewed, and handled situations. He had to begin all over again. Life wasn't just black and white as he had previously thought.

Standing up, he raised his hands to stop Ndidi's protests.

"Doctor, I want to go home now," he said as he stood up from the bed.

Looking around for his shirt and trousers, he watched as his wife ran quickly to get them, sensing what he needed before he even asked. He hated the dutiful wife persona. He was done with being treated like a demi god—it was time they began as partners.

"But, Mr. Ikenna, I still have to run some tests to find out exactly what is going on internally. Because it's a miracle you came out alive and free from any permanent damage."

"Don't worry, Doctor. I have to go home. If I need any medication, please just prescribe them for me." Stretching out his hands, he continued. "You can see that I am fine. I do not know how I got healed, but I am fine," he finished.

After some more minutes spent going back and forth with the doctor who was trying to get him to stay in the hospital longer, the man finally gave up, warning him that he must sign a self-discharge document before leaving the hospital, declaring that he was the one who'd ordered his discharge.

After signing the papers, Ikenna picked up his bag, letting his wife know that he could carry it, and walked out of the hospital.

"Where are my friends?" he asked as soon as they got into the car, stilling himself to hear the worst.

"It's unbelievable, but they, too, survived. In fact, Nonso wasn't even admitted into the hospital at all," Ndidi finished.

Grateful that his friends had survived, Ikenna knew it was time to make a decision about his life, and fast, too. Adjusting his car seat, he leaned back and closed his eyes, remaining silent 'til they got home, grateful for the lack of traffic.

"Ikenna, you have changed."

He sat down on the parlor sofa as soon as they got inside the house. "How do you mean, Ndidi?"

He could sense that he had changed, not physically as he was now in his body, but he truly had changed. He didn't need a soothsayer to tell him this, but it wasn't going to be the same between Ndidi and himself. He needed to get to truly know her.

He had to begin dating his wife all over again. He couldn't even remember evenings of just talking well into the night, getting to know each other when they were just dating. They both felt like strangers, moreso himself, because Ndidi knew at least all the things he liked. On the other hand, he couldn't even tell what her favorite meal was or her favorite colour.

"Ndidi, what are the things you like to do, like a hobby?"

She seemed surprised. "What do you mean? I don't have any hobbies. My life is all about you and the kids. Why do you think I was devastated when you had the accident; you were the only one who was unconscious. I thought I was going to lose you."

"Where are the kids now?" he asked.

Ndidi didn't understand him. He hoped he wasn't the one who had made it this way. What he couldn't understand was why she'd let him take hold of her life in the first place. Thinking of Nkechi again—she had a lot of similiarities with his Ndidi—an ache started in his heart. They had both gone through a lot purely because they'd been born females.

"I have sent them to go and stay with my mother. Do you want me to go and get them?" Ndidi asked, sitting down on the sofa opposite him.

Ikenna's first thought was to demand that his kids be brought back home.

"What do *you* want, Ndidi?" he asked.

The way her eyes grew big in disbelief made him chuckle.

"I don't really know." Ndidi hesistated. "I mean… they can stay a few days at my mum's place."

"Okay," Ikenna responded.

Looking around at the sitting room, he loathed the décor. Why did they have all these things around? They had about five television sets, all around the parlor. He knew that only one of the televisions was working, the one placed at the center of the sitting room. In one corner of the room, there were piles of old newspapers scattered around, and furthermore, children's toys in another corner.

"Are all the television sets in this parlor working?"

"No, they are not, but you never wanted to remove them, and they have been here for a while," Ndidi replied. "Do you want to watch anything, the news, sports, or a movie? I can put it on for you," she fussed.

"Don't worry, Ndidi. Forget about what I want, and what I need. I want to talk about you. You cannot tell me that you do not have any hobbies. What do you like to do in your spare time, and please don't be afraid of telling me the truth, I can take it," he finished.

She looked at him suspiciously. "I have always been interested in cars. As a young girl, I used to dream of owning a car manufacturing company. Mercedes Benz is my type of car any day any time, but it's all a dream. It can never happen." She sighed.

"Why do you say so?" Ikenna asked.

He had never been so surprised. He would never have thought his wife was interested in cars. In fact, in all the fifteen years that they had been married, he had only seen her drive occassionally. Most times, she would always opt for the public transport.

"Why are you asking as though you don't know? It's not a profession for a woman."

"So what is a profession for a woman?" he asked, curious to hear what she would say.

"Teaching in a primary school, for instance."

"Is that why you became a teacher?" he asked, flummoxed.

"Yes. That was why I did it. Don't get me wrong, teaching is a very noble job and shouldn't just be for women, but it is not my passion, and I hate it. I can't stand it. I can't stand the kids. If I had my way, I would never have had three kids. Please don't get me wrong, Ikenna. I love my children, our children, but that is as far as it gets."

Studying his wife again, he realized that he truly didn't know her. He was seeing a side of her that he hadn't seen in fifteen years, or ever at all. She didn't like her work, and he would have thought that she did, as she was always the first to get to work and the last to leave. He knew she didn't want a lot of children, but then, he had been selfish, and her mother, as well, didn't help matters, scolding her anytime she complained about giving birth to more kids. Her mother always told her to shut her mouth and listen to her husband as he was more intelligent than her.

At the time, he hadn't seen it as an issue; he'd felt what his mother-in-law said was the right thing. But now, looking at her, he realized how wrong he had been. He had tried to mould this woman into something she wasn't.

Even if she stayed by his side, he knew that she was just a bubble waiting to explode one day.

"If that is what you want to do, then I think you should go for it."

She stood up. "*Ha!* Ikenna, you don't know what you are saying. I am already an old woman. I cannot do that again, and above all, what will people say?"

"No, you aren't. You haven't even turned forty, and who says you cannot do what you want? You can, and I want you to start right now. From now on, do things that please you and not me."

"Let me get you your food," she replied and walked to the kitchen, for lack of what to say.

Ikenna knew she was running away. She wanted to clear her head. He couldn't blame her—his behavior was very strange, and this wasn't the Ikenna she knew. He couldn't believe that he had been a dictator; he had oppressed his wife. He couldn't change the past, but he could certainly change the future, and he was going to start with his wife and kids. First, he had to make sure that they were well taken care of, in case something tragic befell him.

Walking slowly, he found Ndidi. She was bent down, looking through the pots, as though trying to select a special one. He had always liked the shape of her bum and had never said anything about it. Compliments weren't his forte, but yet, as humans, we all craved it, at least from our loved ones.

"You do not need to worry about what I will eat. I would have made something for both of us, seeing the kids are away". Raising his hands up in the air, he continued. "Unfortunately, I cannot cook, a skill which I should learn. At least the basics."

Again, Ndidi looked at him in surprise, and then, the tears started rolling down. She slid to the floor and just wrapped her arms around her as she cried.

Walking towards her, he sat down beside her and let the tears roll down. Staring at him again looking flummoxed, she wiped her face as she stared.

He smiled. "Yeah, I know you've never seen me cry. I am crying now, and it's the most uncomfortable thing ever seeing that my wife looks at me in a strange way," he finished, and they both chuckled.

Taking her hands in his, he sighed and looked at her. "Ndidi, I need to apologise for what I have done to you in the past. It's almost as though I let my insecurities dictate the pace in this marriage."

Taking his thumb, he caressed her lips. Reaching forward, he gave her a light kiss. The tightness he felt was surreal. He wanted more, but it was time to pace himself.

Ikenna watched as she brought her fingers to her lips. He wanted to climb to the top of the highest mountain and shout like a caveman that he still got it in him, but he restrained himself.

"Babe, I have done a lot of things in the past which I shouldn't have, and I am so sorry for that. I wish I had listened to you a long time ago, asked for your opinions about different things, everything that concerns us. Look around you. This house isn't your taste or style, is it?"

Ndidi nodded.

"I knew it", he continued. "A lot of things happened to me when I was in a coma. I am not sure you are even going to believe me, but rest assured that I will let you know one day, and this has changed me for the better."

"So are you saying that we are going our separate ways?" Ndidi asked as she gently pulled her hands away from his.

The turmoil Ikenna felt within could have destroyed a whole planet. He didn't think that it was going to be easy, but he thought he was going to be given a chance at least to prove himself.

"Is that what you want?" he asked, petrified.

She looked down. "Not really. I used to love you once, Ikenna, but right now, I do not even know."

Looking at him, she continued. "I do not know where the boldness has come from, for me, but I guess maybe seeing you in that hospital bed brought everything into perspective."

Moving closer to Ndidi, he leaned his head on her shoulder. "I know I have messed up big time, and I am ready to learn. I have been a horrible person, and I am ashamed of all that I have put you through. I want us to begin again. Just a day at a time. Please give me another chance?"

"What really happened to you? Did you go to Hell or something?" Ndidi asked.

Ikenna laughed. "Let's just say that realizing that you have been an ungrateful bastard isn't a good thing to find out about yourself."

She wrapped her arms around him. "I am not sure I can love you again, but I will try and give us another chance since you are willing. Please take it slow with me this time." Ndidi sighed.

"I will, babe."

RESOLUTIONS

It had been a journey for both of them. When Ndidi said she wanted him to take her time, she had really meant it. Ikenna has never worked as hard in his life as he was currently. It had taken them a lot to get to this point. He actually got to know a lot of things about Ndidi that he never knew about her, and she vice versa.

His kids could even sense the change in him. He wasn't shouting all the time. Now, they had conversations. He had told Ndidi about Nkechi and his quest to find her and looking for ways to help her. He'd told her everything and how it had been a healing process. 'Til now, he hadn't been able to find Nkechi or Doris or what happened to the baby and her horrible in-laws.

He also wanted to thank Nkechi for what Fate had given him, because he would have lost everything he'd worked for if he hadn't had the accident.

Ikenna knew that he never wanted to find himself in a woman's body again. Every now and then, he would put his hands inside his trousers to feel his penis. He would pat it and thank his stars that he had it back, safe and sound.

Ndidi laughed at him when she found out he did that. He was just happy, he responded. Another time he had to specifically thank the gods was when he finally made love to Ndidi after what felt like an eternity. It was bliss. This time around, he let her lead. Who would have thought that his Ndidi liked to be a leader and he liked to be led? It was a whole new experience. The different parts of his body she discovered that pleasured him amused and amazed him. Ndidi was on a mission, and he loved it.

Slowly, they had learnt to become transparent and vulnerable with each other, which had in turned helped their relationship. In time, he would find Nkechi and Doris. In time, he would be able to help these women, and in his own way, make an impact.

***

It was a challenging healing process for Nkechi right now. She found it difficult to concentrate when she kept having the same dreams over and over again, and lately, the dreams had been somewhat different.

Yesterday, for instance, she'd dreamt that not only was she running away from something or someone, she was also screaming. She'd felt it, a dark spirit running after her and laughing as she tried to get away. She'd heard a child screaming her name, calling her, "*Mama, please come and help me.*" But as she ran towards the direction of the voice, she slipped and fell into a lake. She knew how to swim, but for some reason in her dream, she could not swim.

She was struggling in the water, and the more she opened her mouth to scream for help, the more she gulped in a lot of water. She tried any which way she could, but to no avail. Then, she felt someone grab hold of her. She knew they were calling out to her, but she couldn't pick out a word the stranger was saying. She was stuck in time.

Suddenly, she could see herself in a tunnel, and there was a bright light at the end of it. But when she looked back, it was very dark. She wanted to walk towards the bright light, but she was trapped. It was as though her feet were in quicksand, and she knew she was going to die.

The stranger kept trying to resuscitate her. It was a bit of a dilemma because even though she was stuck in the middle of the tunnel, she didn't think she wanted to be resuscitated. A part of her wanted to be in this unknown world forever while the other part of her wanted to go home with the stranger whose touch was comforting.

It was at this point she had woken up from her sleep. She knew something strange had occurred during the burial of Godwin, but she couldn't really pinpoint what it was.

All the words she had heard had been that she should begin a new life of her own. She had lost the baby due to a minor accident, but with everything that unfolded with Godwin's in-laws, in a way, she was happy she had cut all ties with him.

But beginning a new life was easier said than done. Her friend Doris has been a shelter and good friend and sister, but even she couldn't comfort her at nights.

She had to grow up. Put on big girl's panties and face the world headlong. Doris had kind of discouraged her a bit, saying that the world was unfair to widows, but she wasn't going to let it happen. She was going to push and continue pushing 'til she conquered every obstacle in her way. In the meantime, she would have to work through her dreams.

Help was out there—she could feel it. She would wait for it to come.

Thank you for reading!
Remember to leave a review.
Connect with Firi Kamson:
Facebook.com/me.FiriKamson
Twitter.com/tmkamson
Instagram.com/firikamson

OTHER BOOKS BY LOVE AFRICA PRESS

Queer and Sexy Collection Vol 1 by Eniitan

Be My Valentine Anthology Vol 1 by Amaka Azie, Fiona Khan, Nana Prah, Sable Rose, Empi Baryeh

His Captive Princess by Kiru Taye

CONNECT WITH US

Facebook.com/LoveAfricaPress

Twitter.com/LoveAfricaPress

Instagram.com/LoveAfricaPress

www.loveafricapress.com